Linda Lael Miller ... frontier her own s... more so than in this heartwarming new series that brings four women west to share an inheritance—2,500 acres of timber and high-country grassland called Primrose Creek.

In this wonderful new series, four cousins discover the dangers and the joys, the hardship and the beauty, of frontier life. And each, in her own way, finds a love that will last an eternity. Join with the McQuarry women in a special celebration of the love, courage, and family ties that made the West great.

Four special women. Four extraordinary stories.

THE WOMEN OF
PRIMROSE CREEK

BRIDGET

CHRISTY

SKYE

MEGAN

Praise for Linda Lael Miller's bestselling series

SPRINGWATER SEASONS

"A DELIGHTFUL AND DELICIOUS MINI-SERIES. . . . *Rachel* will charm you, enchant you, delight you, and quite simply hook you. . . . *Miranda* is a sensual marriage-of-convenience tale guaranteed to warm your heart all the way down to your toes. . . . The warmth that spreads through *Jessica* is captivating. . . . The gentle beauty of the tales and the delightful, warmhearted characters bring a slice of Americana straight onto readers' 'keeper' shelves. Linda Lael Miller's miniseries is a gift to treasure."

—*Romantic Times*

"This hopeful tale is . . . infused with the sensuality that Miller is known for."

—*Booklist*

"All the books in this collection have the Linda Lael Miller touch."

—*Affaire de Coeur*

"Nobody brings the folksiness of the Old West to life better than Linda Lael Miller."

—*BookPage*

"Another warm, tender story from the ever-so-talented pen of one of this genre's all-time favorites."

—*Rendezvous*

"Miller . . . create[s] a warm and cozy love story."

—*Publishers Weekly*

Acclaim for Linda Lael Miller's irresistible novels of love in the Wild West

SPRINGWATER

"Heartwarming. . . . Linda Lael Miller captures not only the ambiance of a small Western town, but the need for love, companionship, and kindness that is within all of us. . . . *Springwater* is what Americana romance is all about."
—*Romantic Times*

"A heartwarming tale with adorable and endearing characters."
—*Rendezvous*

A SPRINGWATER CHRISTMAS

"A tender and beautiful story. . . . Christmas is the perfect time of year to return to Springwater Station and the unforgettable characters we've come to know and love. . . . Linda Lael Miller has once more given us a gift of love."
—*Romantic Times*

THE VOW

"The Wild West comes alive through the loving touch of Linda Lael Miller's gifted words. . . . Breathtaking. . . . A romantic masterpiece. This one is a keeper you'll want to take down and read again and again."
—*Rendezvous*

"A beautiful tale of love lost and regained. . . . A magical Western romance . . . that would be a masterpiece in any era."
—Amazon.com

Books by Linda Lael Miller

Banner O'Brien
Corbin's Fancy
Memory's Embrace
My Darling Melissa
Angelfire
Desire and Destiny
Fletcher's Woman
Lauralee
Moonfire
Wanton Angel
Willow
Princess Annie
The Legacy
Taming Charlotte
Yankee Wife
Daniel's Bride
Lily and the Major
Emma and the Outlaw
Caroline and the Raider
Pirates
Knights
My Outlaw
The Vow
Two Brothers
Springwater
Springwater Season series:
- Rachel
- Savannah
- Miranda
- Jessica

A Springwater Christmas
One Wish
The Women of Primrose Creek series:
- Bridget
- Christy

Linda Lael Miller

The Women of Primrose Creek

Christy

SONNET BOOKS
New York London Toronto Sydney Singapore

This book is a work of fiction. Names, characters, places and incidents are products of the author's imagination or are used fictitiously. Any resemblance to actual events or locales or persons, living or dead, is entirely coincidental.

An *Original* Publication of POCKET BOOKS

A Sonnet Book published by
POCKET BOOKS, a division of Simon & Schuster Inc.
1230 Avenue of the Americas, New York, NY 10020

ISBN: 0-671-04245-9

First Sonnet Books printing June 2000

10 9 8 7 6 5 4 3 2 1

Cover art by Robert Hunt

Printed in the U.S.A.

For Ramona Stratton, with love.
From here out, it's all good.

Christy

Prologue

Fort Grant, Nevada
1868

With no small amount of trepidation, Christy McQuarry peered through the late Mrs. Royd's limp lace curtains, assessing the man sent to fetch them home to Primrose Creek. It had been alarming enough, during the long, dull winter passed at Fort Grant, to consider putting herself, Caney, and especially Megan, her younger sister, in the charge of some mere passerby for the remainder of the journey. A grizzled old prospector, for example, or one of the seedy-looking scouts who came and went on occasion, foul-smelling and full of horrendous tales involving Indians and outlaws. For some indefinable reason, she found this particular man, fair-haired and blue-eyed, insolently handsome in his ordinary but obviously clean clothes and well-worn hat, almost equally disturbing. He rode a splendid cocoa-brown stallion with a pale mane and tail, and a .45 caliber pistol rested low and easy on his left hip, seemingly as much a part of him as a finger or a foot.

"I don't like him," she confided to Caney Blue, the tall and angular black woman who had worked on the McQuarry farm, back in Virginia, for as long as Christy's memory reached. Which, since she was nearly twenty, was a considerable distance. "He's too handsome. Too sure of himself."

Caney was smiling her broad and luminous smile, watching as the man dismounted and offered a hand and a grin to the aging army officer who had gone out to greet him. "That so?" she said, her dark eyes following the man as he spoke with the colonel in the street just beyond the window of the modest parlor. There was precisely one house at Fort Grant, if indeed such a rustic structure could be described as a house, and it belonged to the recently widowed commander of the installation, Colonel Webley Royd, who had kindly given the place over to the women upon their arrival the previous October with the first flurries of snow. "Well, I think he's right purty. And I like a man who thinks well of himself."

A star-shaped badge glinted on the front of the visitor's shirt, and Christy clamped her back teeth together for a moment, without quite knowing why a stranger should affect her so. She might have been struck by a runaway freight car, so great and so confounding was the impact of merely *seeing* him. What would it be like to actually meet him? To travel in his company?

"Colonel Royd told me his name is Zachary Shaw," Megan put in eagerly, from her post on the other side of the window. Being just sixteen, she could not be expected, Christy supposed, to exhibit any real degree of good judgment. She had a headful of dreams, Megan did, and at the same time one of the finest minds Christy had ever encountered. She meant to see that her sister didn't waste that gift by settling for a house and a husband and a half dozen babies, which she feared Megan was wont to do. "He's a U.S. Marshal."

He's trouble, Christy thought to herself. At just that moment, as if to confirm this opinion, Marshal Zachary Shaw seemed to sense her perusal; his gaze met and captured hers through the gauzy veil of lace. Held it fast.

Infuriated, and stirred in a way that was not entirely proper, Christy glared at him, in hopes of hiding the fact that she could not look away until he chose to release her.

He grinned and tugged at the brim of his shapeless hat, and Christy felt a sudden, primitive sort of heat pounding in all her pulses, throbbing in her face.

"Well, I'll be," Caney remarked in a murmur. Caney could be damnably perceptive at times.

Christy somehow gathered the strength to step back from the window and whirl away on one heel. "He won't do," she blustered, pacing at the edge of a hand-hooked rug. "He simply won't do. He's arrogant, and almost certainly a rascal. We'll have to find someone else to escort us. Or make the trip on our own."

Megan turned to stare at her sister, appalled. With her auburn hair, flawless skin, and Irish-green eyes,

Megan was a stunning beauty, though, despite her brilliance, a naive child in so many ways. From the day they left Virginia for the first time, amid the scandal of their parents' acrimonious divorce, life had consisted of one loss, one humiliation, one defeat after another, but things were going to be different from here on, if Christy had any say in the matter. And she had plenty.

"Christy!" Megan marveled. "You can't be serious—it's miles and miles to Primrose Creek, and there are wild animals, and road agents, and renegade Indians—"

Caney was already shaking her head. "You've done gone fool-headed if you think we're goin' up into them mountains on our own," she vowed. During the trip west, she'd often allowed Christy to help her tend the sick and injured, and once she'd even helped to deliver a baby. Caney had told Christy she had a gift for healing, but most of the time—like now—the woman treated her as if she were still a child.

Christy didn't relish the thought of another perilous journey herself, but pride usually compelled her to stand her ground in the face of any opposition, and that warm spring afternoon was no exception. "Good heavens," she said in a hissing whisper, "we traveled all the way from Virginia, didn't we?"

"We was with a wagon train," Caney pointed out, just as impatiently.

Megan's eyes were enormous with memories of the voyage, many of which were unpleasant ones. They'd been through so much in the past few years, first being dragged away from the family to England, then being sent back again over tempestuous seas, only to reach Virginia and find that their grandfather, Gideon McQuarry, had died, as had both their father and uncle, and the farm was gone forever. They were essentially penniless now, she and Megan, and the tract of land at Primrose Creek, an inheritance from Granddaddy, to be shared equally with their cousins, Bridget and Skye, represented their best hope of gaining a foothold.

"He looks strong," Megan said at last. Hopefully. "Marshal Shaw, I mean."

"Ain't that the truth of it," Caney commented, still watching him through the window. "Knows how to take care of himself, a body can see that right off."

"And us, too," Megan pressed.

Christy let out a long sigh. She would put aside her personal misgivings—hadn't she done that often enough to become expert at it?—and go along with what Megan and Caney wanted. "All right," she breathed. "All right. We'll travel with the marshal." *But no good will come of it,* she added, to herself.

Colonel Royd brought the lawman to supper that evening, and they all sat down to one of Caney's legendary fried chicken dinners. Although she tried not to fidget, Christy was unsettled throughout the meal, and her appetite, usually unshakable, was nonexistent. Little wonder; she was seated directly across from the marshal, by some contrivance of Caney's, and when he looked at her with those bright blue eyes, she felt as though her deepest secrets were written on her skin.

Worse, he had taken notice of her discomfiture, and—just *imagine*—it made him smile a very small, very private, twitch-at-the-corner type of smile.

"Have you lived at Primrose Creek long, Mr. Shaw?" she asked, her hands knotted in her lap, just to show him he hadn't had any affect whatsoever upon her. Which, of course, he had.

He lifted one finely made shoulder in a semblance of a shrug. "No, ma'am," he said. "Fact is, I was just passing through, and I got into a poker game over at the Silver Spike. I lost, as it happens."

"You lost?" Christy echoed, mystified, and immediately wished she'd held her tongue. Odd, how this man perturbed her. If there was one thing Christy prided herself on, it was her ability to retain her emotional balance, yet he made her feel as though she were dancing on a rolling log in the middle of a raging river. "I don't see what that has to do with anything."

Again, that grin, so boyish and yet so grown-up. So certain of himself and his ability to make his way in the world. "No, ma'am," he said easily. "I don't reckon you would." He paused, took a breath and another of Caney's biscuits. His third, Christy noted. "My old friend Sam Flynn was wearing this badge then. He wanted to head down to Virginia City and try his luck in the mines for a year or so, but he couldn't find anybody willing to serve out his term. He suckered me into a poker game, and, well, like I said, I lost. Fact is, I'm not exactly sure he didn't stack the deck."

The colonel gave his booming laugh. He was a pleasant, somewhat corpulent man, fond of Caney's cooking. Indeed, he'd tried to persuade her to stay and keep house for him there at Fort Grant, and certainly Christy couldn't have blamed the woman if she'd agreed, considering that the position offered a salary along with room and board. All she and Megan had to offer was their friendship.

"That would be like Sam," Royd said, serving himself another helping of mashed potatoes. "If I were you, Shaw, I wouldn't look for him to come back—especially if he strikes it rich in the Comstock."

Mr. Shaw gave a rueful sigh. "If he doesn't show up when he's supposed to," he said, "I might just have to hunt him down and shoot him."

A brief silence descended, while everyone else at the table, Christy suspected, tried to decide whether or not he was serious. His expression, while affable enough and certainly polite, gave nothing away.

Then the colonel laughed again, thunderously, all but shaking the crockery on the table. Clearly, he thought the marshal was joking. Caney chuckled, a bit belatedly, and Megan twittered a little, her gaze resting adoringly upon Zachary Shaw.

Christy, however, was not amused, for it seemed to her that the marshal had spoken in all seriousness. "When will we set out for Primrose Creek?" she asked, without smiling.

"Dawn," Mr. Shaw answered. He wasn't smiling, either. It seemed to Christy in that moment that they understood each other, for good or for ill. "I'll want to load the wagon tonight. Everything is packed, I assume?"

"Such as it is," Caney put in, while Christy was strangling on a civil answer of her own.

"Good," he said, still watching Christy. His gaze had not strayed from her face, she realized, in some moments. "It's a hard trip, and it's dangerous. We'll be two days on the road, at the least. I'm in charge until we get there, and I'll thank everybody to remember that."

There was another silence, during which Christy tried to stare him down, let him know who was boss. In the end, though, it was she who looked away.

Zachary passed the night in the soldiers' barracks and soon found that he was the envy of every man there, just because he was squiring the women back up the mountain to Primrose Creek.

Lying on his back on a cot, his hands cupped behind his head as he settled in to sleep, he listened.

"That dark-haired one, Miss Christy," ventured one soldier, after the last lamp was extinguished, "she's pretty as a china doll. Mean, though."

Zachary felt a tightening in his gut, though he grinned into the darkness. "She's got the temperament of a wet cat, all right," he allowed.

Another voice piped up. "Ain't like we didn't try to court her, every last one of us. She's too fancy for the likes of us, though—made that right plain. In fact, she as good as told Jim Toth to his face that there's nobody here to suit her. Didn't she, Jim?"

"Yup," someone, probably Jim, replied mournfully. "She comes from money and property. All you got to do is look at her to know that. Said she's got to think of her future, and her sister's."

Zachary's smile faded, though he couldn't have said why he took to feeling gloomy all of a sudden. It wasn't as if he gave a damn about Christy McQuarry.

"Yup. Someone's probably [illegible]," replied [illegible] resentfully. "She comes from money [illegible]. All she's got to do is look at her to know that. And she's got to think of her future, and her sister's."

[illegible] smile faded, although he couldn't have said why he took to feeling glum all of a sudden. It wasn't as if he gave a damn about Cherry McMurry.

Chapter 1

"There it is," the marshal said, with obvious relief, doffing his hat to indicate a meandering stream, winking with silvery patches of sunlight as it flowed across the valley tucked amid the peaks of the High Sierras. Trees bristled on all sides, ponderosa pine and Douglas fir mostly, so dense that they appeared more blue than green, though there were splashes of aspen and maple, oak and cottonwood here and there. "That's Primrose Creek. The town's over yonder, about two miles southwest of here."

Christy stood in her stirrups and drew in a sharp breath. The air was soft with the promise of a warm summer, and the view was so spectacular that it made her heart catch and brought the sting of tears to her eyes.

Megan, riding beside her, drew in a breath and then exclaimed, "It's Beulah Land!" She pointed eagerly. "And look—that must be Bridget and Skye's house, there by the bend in the stream. Oh, Christy, isn't it grand?"

Some of Christy's own delight in their arrival faded. She and Megan had passed the war years in Great Britain, at the insistence of their mother, Jenny Davis McQuarry, who had kicked up considerable dust back in Virginia by leaving her drunken rounder of a husband, Eli, and running off with a titled Englishman. Jenny's new love, a relatively minor baron as it turned out, and not an earl as he had led her to believe, was nonetheless the master of Fieldcrest, a small estate in the heart of Devon. He had promptly sent both his bride's daughters off to St. Martha's, a boarding school outside London—over Jenny's anemic protests—and had never made a secret of the fact that he would have preferred to leave them behind with their ruffian relatives in the first place. When Jenny had died suddenly of a fever in the winter of 1866, he'd been quick to pack them off to America.

Christy would have been overjoyed to return, except that by then they had almost no family left; their father and Uncle J.R. had both been killed in the War between the States, and their passage had been booked when word of their beloved grandfather's death reached them in the form of a terse letter from Gideon McQuarry's lawyers. Already grief-stricken at her mother's passing, and now Gideon's, Christy had been in a private panic. She'd succeeded in putting on a brave front, for Megan's sake, and had impetuously written her cousin Bridget, an act she would soon regret, offering to sell their half of the inheritance, hers and Megan's, as outlined in the copy of Gideon

McQuarry's will. There had not been enough time for a response from Bridget before their ship sailed, and, besides, she did not have the right to dispose of Megan's share of the bequest in the same way as her own. With only their clothes—including ugly school uniforms and a few ball gowns garnered from their mother's wardrobe—a set of china that had belonged to their grandmother Rebecca, and the few modest jewels Jenny had managed to acquire during her two tempestuous marriages, they crossed the sea and arrived in Virginia to find strangers living in the house they had loved. Granddaddy was buried in the family plot, alongside the beautiful wife who had died in a riding accident when the girls were small. Uncle J.R. rested beside his father, his grave marked with an impressive granite stone declaring him a Union hero. Christy and Megan's father, Eli, lay next to Rebecca, but a little apart from the others, or so it seemed to Christy. He had fought bravely, his wooden marker claimed, under the direct command of General Robert E. Lee.

There had been no reason to stay in Virginia, with everything and everyone they loved gone.

"Ma'am?" the marshal prompted, bringing Christy back from her musings with a snap. He was about thirty years of age, she estimated, though she'd been doing her best, ever since they'd left Fort Grant that morning not to think of him at all. He was easy in his skin, with a habit of whistling cheerfully, and just being near him made Christy feel breathless and off-balance, as though the ground had been jerked from beneath her feet. She had expected these emotions to pass while they were traveling together, especially since they had disagreed practically every time they had occasion to speak, but they had only intensified, and she blamed him entirely. "I reckon we ought to ride on down there and let them know you're here."

Behind Christy and the marshal, Caney waited at the reins of a wagon she'd driven all the way from Virginia. Also known as Miz Blue, Caney had been at the farm when Christy and Megan arrived from England; she and her man, Titus, had worked for Granddaddy as free people, since he'd never kept slaves. Recently widowed and "frightful lonesome," Caney had chosen to accompany them on the trip west to the spanking new state of Nevada—the state whose wealth of silver had helped to finance the Union cause. "Yez, Missy," she said now. "This here wagon seat be harder than the devil's heart. I want to sit me down someplace comfortable!"

Christy turned her head and gave her friend a narrow look. The daughter of a Baptist preacher, Caney had learned to read and write before she was six, and her grammar was as good as anybody's. Still, she liked to carry on like an ignorant bond servant once in a while, for reasons she had never troubled herself to share.

Caney met Christy's gaze straight on, and without flinching. Her mannish jaw was set, and her dark eyes glittered with challenge. "I will surely be glad to look upon Miss Bridget and Miss Skye again," she said. "They's my own precious babies, just like you and Miss Megan. Oh, I will be glad, indeed."

Megan was flushed and beaming at the prospect of a family reunion, and Marshal Zachary Shaw was obviously chafing to get on with whatever it was he did to keep the peace in the town of Primrose Creek. It seemed that Christy was quite alone in her reluctance to come face-to-face with their Yankee cousins. She hoped neither Caney nor Megan remembered the last time she and Bridget had been together; they'd gotten into a hissing, scratching, screeching fight, right there in the front yard at the farm, and would surely have killed each other if Uncle J.R. and a laughing Trace hadn't hauled them apart and held them till they were too exhausted from kicking and struggling to go at it again.

"I declare a place as grand as that *must* have a bathtub," Megan mused, squinting a little in the bright spring sunshine. Then, as if that decided the matter, she spurred the little pinto pony she was riding, on loan from the army as was the spirited sorrel gelding Christy had been assigned, down the trail toward the rambling log house, with its glistening glass windows and smoking chimneys. Caney headed that way, too, which left Christy alone on the ridge with Mr. Shaw.

She shifted uncomfortably in the saddle, while he swept off his disreputable leather hat to run one forearm across his forehead. In spite of herself, and all her efforts to ignore him, she was aware of the man in every sense. He was in his shirtsleeves, having shed his heavy coat earlier and bound it behind his saddle with strands of rawhide, and his suspenders were exposed. His shoulders and chest were broad, tapering to a lean waist, and his hair, the color of new straw, wanted cutting. His eyes seemed to see past all the barriers Christy had erected over the years, and that alone would have been reason enough to avoid him, but there was much more to the allure than that. Indeed, it had an almost mystical quality, not merely physical but a thing of the soul and the spirit as well.

"You'll be all right now," he said, and Christy couldn't tell whether he was making a statement or asking a question. In the end, she didn't care, or so she told herself. She just wanted to see the back of Zachary Shaw, once and for all. Bad enough she'd had to put up with him for three days and two nights on the trail.

"Yes," she replied, as stiffly as if she'd been addressing a scullery maid in the kitchen at Fieldcrest. "Thank you very much, Marshal. You may go now."

His eyes lighted with amazed amusement, and his mouth tilted upward in a cocky grin. "Well, now. That's mighty generous of you, Lady McQuarry," he teased. "Your giving me permission to leave your presence and all."

He'd made no secret of the fact that he thought she was high-handed and uppity, but Christy felt a flood of startled color surge into her face all the same. No matter what she said, he'd probably manage to misconstrue her words, make her seem condescending, even snobbish. Well, she wasn't going to let him have the satisfaction of upsetting her any more than he already had.

"Good day," she said, tartly this time.

He chuckled, shook his head again, reined his spectacular cocoa-colored stallion around, and rode off toward the southwest without slowing down or looking back. For some thoroughly unaccountable reason, she was disappointed.

Quite against her will, let alone her better judgment, Christy watched him until he disappeared into a grove of cottonwood trees, their leaves shimmering in the breeze like silver coins stitched to a gypsy's skirt, and she had an awful feeling that he knew it. Well, tit for tat, she thought. She'd certainly caught him watching *her* often enough during the trip from Fort Grant, his face a study in perplexed annoyance.

At last, she decided she'd been stalling in order to avoid the inevitable meeting with Bridget and rode slowly down the steep grade, following Megan, who was traveling at a lope now that she'd reached flatter ground, and Caney, rattling along in their ancient mule-drawn wagon, a relic of better days at the farm. There was no sense in putting it off any longer.

When proper greetings had been exchanged, she'd ride over and have a look at her and Megan's side of the creek, decide where they might put up a cabin of some sort to shelter them until they could afford a real house.

Bridget was standing in the doorway now, her abundant hair, as pale as Christy's was dark, swept up at her nape in a loose chignon. She was wearing a blue calico dress that matched her eyes—Christy's were charcoal gray—and she was sumptuously pregnant. She laughed as Megan jumped down from the pinto's back, hurrying toward her like a filly gamboling through a field, and took the girl in her arms. Then, weeping and exclaiming for joy, she turned to embrace Caney.

The merriment had already gone on for some time when Skye came rushing across the clearing, basket in hand, overjoyed to see Megan, her old playmate, and Caney, whom neither she nor Bridget had probably expected to see again, ever. Bridget's boy, Noah, stood staunchly at his mother's side. His resemblance to his late father, Bridget's first husband, Mitch, jarred Christy a little. He was four or five, and there was a spark of formidable intelligence in his eyes.

She managed to dismount, but her legs seemed to be sending roots deep into the ground, and she couldn't make herself take a single step forward. When she did contrive to move, it was only to turn and flee. She promptly came face-to-chest with Trace Qualtrough.

She'd known that he and Bridget were married—the marshal had told her in one of their brief, stilted conversations—but that didn't lessen the impact of actually seeing him again. The memory of their last meeting was as much a thorn in her side as that of the scene she and Bridget had made, brawling in the dirt like a pair of tavern wenches. She'd declared her eternal love and begged Trace to wait until she was older; she would come home from England then, and they would be wed. He'd smiled sadly, kissed her forehead, and said he didn't plan to take a wife, ever, and she'd felt as though he'd plunged a knife into her.

Older now, and handsomer than before, if that were possible, he nonetheless had no effect whatsoever on her emotions. She supposed she'd become jaded, reflecting on her father's wild and irresponsible ways and the unfriendly nature of her mother's second husband.

"Running away?" he teased, taking a gentle hold of her shoulders. Trace assessed her with brotherly dispatch and pulled a face. "That isn't like you, Christy. Besides, I believe you might be able take Bridget this time, her being pregnant and all. You'd want to watch out, though. She bites."

Christy laughed, almost giddy with relief that her little-girl adoration for this man was gone. Perhaps the old animosity between herself and Bridget would prove as fleeting, and they could become friends. Or at least establish a truce of some kind. "Have you forgotten that we were practically children at the time?"

"Not for a moment," he replied, and took her elbow lightly in one hand. "Come on. Let's get this done. Bridget's dreading it as much as you are."

To her credit, Bridget met them halfway, wiping her hands unconsciously on her apron as she approached. Her expression was solemn, even wary, but not unfriendly. "Come inside," she said in a quiet voice. "You must be longing for a cup of hot tea."

Christy had been braced for censure; their legendary catfight notwithstanding, she and Bridget had never been close, as Skye and Megan were. Long before their fathers had taken separate sides on the questions of states' rights and secession, they'd bickered over dolls, ponies, lemon tea cakes, and, in time, matters of decorum. Bridget had been a veritable hoyden, a blight upon the McQuarry name, while Christy had endeavored to behave as a lady—most of the time. The only thing they'd had in common, besides the proud, stubborn blood of Gideon and Rebecca McQuarry simmering in their veins, was a deep interest in horses. Both had been expert riders almost from the moment they could sit a horse, and at that point, where they might have found an affinity, they'd become rivals instead.

"Thank you," Christy murmured with a nod. She hadn't enjoyed real tea since she'd left England, for such luxuries were still rare in Virginia and impossibly dear when they could be found. It made her grind her teeth just to think of how poor she and Megan really were, but if she had her way, they'd never have to fear poverty again.

Bridget linked her arm through Christy's and tugged her toward the open doorway. "Tell me," she began, "about the farm. Are the new people diligent? The barn wanted painting when we left—"

The inside of the house was cool and spacious and smelled pleasantly of baking bread. There was a good stove at one end of the large central room, and three doorways led into other parts of the house. A gigantic rock fireplace stood opposite the kitchen area, faced with handmade rocking chairs and a cushioned bench, and just looking around spawned a bittersweet mixture of sorrow and pleasure in Christy. Pleasure because the place reminded her so much of the farmhouse back home in Virginia, and sorrow because it wasn't her house at all, but Bridget's.

Always, Bridget.

"Christy?" Bridget spoke gently. Cautiously.

She glanced back and smiled to see that she and Bridget were alone. Convenient, she thought. No doubt, the others considered themselves peacemakers, even diplomats, giving the two cousins a chance to work out their long-standing differences by staying clear for a while.

"They've put on a new roof," she said, referring to the new residents at the family farm, as though the thread of the conversation had not been dropped. "And I do believe they mean to shore up the stables before there's any painting done."

Bridget ducked her head, sniffled slightly. Of course, she still missed the homeplace, as did Christy. It was a part of them both, that faraway land of gentle hills and blue-green rivers, and it probably always would be. The deed had borne a McQuarry name since the Revolution, though now it belonged to Northerners, fast-talking carpetbaggers who'd strolled in and claimed the place for back taxes.

"Do sit down and rest yourself," Bridget said, without looking at Christy. She hurried to the stove, while Christy took a seat in one of the rocking chairs and stared into the dying fire.

"When is your baby due?" she asked presently. It had taken her that long to come up with a safe topic.

Bridget raised a happy clatter with the teapot, and there was a note of eager anticipation in her voice when she replied. "June," she said. "I'm hoping for a girl, though Trace thinks we ought to have several more sons first, so that our daughters will have older brothers to look after them."

Christy ached with envy, not because Bridget was well married, not even because she was expecting her second child. She was sure to find a husband of her own in a place where women were regarded as a rare treasure, and she would almost certainly have babies, too, in good time. But it was evident that Bridget and Trace had married for love, for passion; she could not expect the same good fortune. No, for Megan's sake, and for her own, Christy was determined to marry for much more practical reasons.

She sat up a little straighter in the rocking chair. "This is a fine home, Bridget," she said. "You've done well."

"Trace deserves most of the credit for the house," Bridget replied lightly, stretching to take a china teapot down from a shelf. "He built it with his own hands. The barn, too."

Christy tilted her head back and looked up at the sturdy log rafters. Perhaps one day, she reflected, this ranch would be to Bridget and Trace's children and grandchildren what the farm had been to several generations of McQuarrys. What legacy might she, Christy, leave to her own descendants?

"Sugar?" Bridget said. "Milk?" It was a moment before Christy, weary of the road, realized her cousin was asking what she took in her tea.

"Just milk," Christy replied. "Please." She studied Bridget as she sat down in the next rocker.

Bridget's spoon rattled as she stirred sugar into her tea. She bit her lower lip once, started to speak, and stopped herself.

"You received my letter?" Christy guessed. "Asking you to buy Megan's and my share of the land?" She paused, savored another sip of tea, stalling. "It was a mistake to make such an offer. I was distraught. I'm—I'm sorry."

Bridget nodded. "I understand," she said. "Still, I'm prepared to pay a fair price. If you're ever of a mind to sell."

Christy set her teacup atop the small table between the two chairs. It nettled her that Bridget not only had Trace, Noah, and the unborn baby but this grand house as well. Even as she spoke, she knew she was being unfair, but she couldn't help herself. Things were so complicated when it came to anything concerning Bridget. "You're not content with the twelve hundred and fifty acres you have here?"

Bridget sat up a little straighter, and a blue tempest ignited in her eyes. "It is not a matter of contentment," she said. "Furthermore, Trace and I own only half of the property, as Skye inherited an equal share. I merely assumed that since you'd written—"

"I told you—I've changed my mind," Christy said as she pushed back her chair a little more forcibly than was required and got to her feet.

Bridget closed her eyes for a moment, in a bid for patience. "Christy, please. Sit down. Hear me out."

Christy began to pace the length of the huge hearth, her arms wrapped tightly around her middle.

"You might as well know it right now. I mean to use that land—my share, anyhow—as a dowry of sorts."

Bridget's mouth dropped open. She looked purely confounded. "A *dowry?*"

"Yes," Christy replied. "Even rich men expect them, you know. In fact, they seem to prefer property over gold or currency, in these uncertain times." She stopped, met Bridget's bewildered gaze. "I mean to marry a wealthy man, for Megan's sake and my own." She threw the words at her cousin's feet like a gauntlet. "The richest one available. Who would that be, Bridget?"

Her cousin's jaw line clamped down hard while she made a visible effort to contain her legendary temper. "If you want to keep the land, that's your right. But only a fool marries for money. I've held many an opinion where you're concerned, Christy McQuarry, but I *never* thought you were a fool."

Christy felt color rise to her face. "I'm not you, Bridget. Lucky stars don't tangle themselves in my hair or fall at my feet—I have to fight for the things I want."

Bridget's own expression softened from anger to sadness. "Christy," she said softly. "It must have been hard, coming home from England—"

"Damn England," Christy spat. "We were miserable there—shunted off and forgotten. Made to feel like poor relations, even beggars."

"Christy," Bridget repeated. "Oh, Christy."

"Don't," Christy said before her cousin could go on. She didn't want Bridget's concern, damn it. Didn't want her pity. She had swallowed enough of her pride already. "You've always been fortune's favorite. You were Granddaddy's favorite, too. And Mitch's. And—Trace's."

"Granddaddy loved you," Bridget insisted. "He was heartbroken to lose you and Megan. He never forgave Jenny for taking you away, or Uncle Eli for letting you go."

Christy did not reply; she would have choked on the painful lump that had risen in her throat. She had never doubted her grandfather's love, as she had her mother's and certainly that of Eli McQuarry, her wild and reckless father. Nor did it particularly trouble her that she would have to make her own way in a world that would grant her no special concessions whatsoever. She had the grit, the strength, the intelligence, and, yes, the beauty to get what she wanted—and she would not be turned from her course.

"Christy," Bridget said once more when she started for the door.

But Christy kept walking and did not look back.

The town of Primrose Creek was hardly more than a cow path with a wide spot, to Zachary's way of thinking, but it had its own sturdy log jailhouse and four saloons. He supposed that said something about a place, that it boasted a hoosegow and more than one watering hole, but no schoolhouse and no real church, either. The Methodists and Baptists held services in borrowed tents, but a hard rain or a high wind could send them scrambling for the shelter of the Silver

Spike, the Golden Garter, the Rip-Snorter, or Diamond Lil's.

Truth to tell, this state of affairs hadn't troubled him much; he wasn't a religious man, despite his good Christian raising, nor was he especially fond of liquor, and had heretofore concerned himself with neither churches nor beer halls. He was even-natured, for the most part, a man with simple wants and wishes. He had a way with horses and little else, and he made a point of minding his own business. Moreover, something had gone cold within him the day Jessie died in his arms, so while he enjoyed a sporting woman as well as the next man, he never thought about settling down.

Now something had changed, and there was no denying it, much as he would have liked to do just that. Some inner foundation had shifted, sent cracks streaking through the walls he'd erected to last a lifetime.

Feeling a chill—spring weather in the Sierras was a fickle thing—he shoved a piece of wood into the stove near his desk and prodded it into flames with the poker. A day ago, he'd showed up at Fort Grant, looking to do his duty as marshal, fetch a gaggle of women safely up the trail, and be done with it. He'd gone, however grudgingly, but the man who'd ridden back up the track wasn't the same as the one who'd ridden down it. And what had wreaked all this havoc? One look at Miss Christy McQuarry, that was what.

He'd seen pretty girls before, of course, even out

there in the back of beyond, but Christy—Miss McQuarry—was more than pretty. She was beautiful. That first sight of her, with her gleaming dark hair and charcoal-gray eyes, her perfect skin and slim, womanly figure, had struck him with the force of a log shooting off one end of a flume, and he was still reeling. God in heaven, he even liked fighting with her.

He rubbed his beard-stubbled chin and squinted into the cracked shaving mirror next to the window. He didn't *look* all that different, but he was thinking some crazy thoughts, that was for sure. He wanted to dance, for God's sake, and not with one of the ladies who plied their trade over at the Golden Garter, either. He wanted an excuse to put his arms around Christy McQuarry, that was a fact, and the music was optional. Furthermore, he'd started to imagine what it would be like, living in a real house with curtains at the windows, raising a passel of kids, just as his own mother and father had done.

He made twenty dollars a month, he reminded himself, and that was when the town council had the funds to pay him, which was only intermittently. He felt his forehead with the back of one hand and grinned ruefully at his own image in the looking glass. No fever.

At least, not in his head.

Christy faced the ramshackle structure with as much courage as she could muster. According to Trace, the place had originally been a Paiute lodge. It had a leaky hide roof, stitched more with daylight than rawhide, and he and Bridget had kept horses there in inclement weather. They'd lived in the place, too, while their house was being built, but Christy took small comfort in that knowledge.

"You must be outta yo' head," Caney said, hands on her hips. "Miss Bridget and Mister Trace have that nice house over yonder, and you want to live here?"

Christy turned to face the woman she considered her only true friend, exasperating as she was. "Go ahead and stay with them, if that's what you want," she replied, keeping her voice crisp.

"Well, I ought to, that's fo' sure. They got real beds over there. They got windows and a roof that don't show no sky through it—"

Determined, Christy began sweeping out the rock-lined fire pit in the center of the building, using a broom she'd improvised herself from twigs and slender branches, and she was brisk about it. "Fine. You're getting old, and you need your comforts. Besides, you got spoiled living at Fort Grant all winter."

Caney rose to the bait like a trout leaping for a fly, and Christy, having her back to the woman now, smiled to herself. "What you mean, I'm gettin' old and spoilt? I ain't but forty-two, and I can do the work of any two mule-skinners. Got you and Miss Megan across all them plains and mountains, didn't I?"

"You did," Christy said, and pressed her lips together.

"You think I ain't got the gumption to sleep in a place like this? Laid my head down in many a worse one, I have."

Christy smiled, swept, and said nothing.

"Drat it all," Caney groused. "You know dern well Miss Megan will stay here if you do, out of plain loyalty, and that leaves me with no choice at all, because I wouldn't sleep a wink for thinkin' of the wolves and the outlaws and the Injuns gettin' to you, after all I done went through to bring you here—"

Shame jabbed at Christy's conscience; she'd promised herself that she wouldn't be like her mother, wouldn't use other people to get her own way, wouldn't use another's weakness to her advantage, and here she was, doing precisely those things. "I'm sorry," she said, turning and meeting Caney's level gaze. "I shouldn't have said anything. I was trying to influence you—"

Caney gave a guffaw of laughter. "Were you, now?" she said, her bright jet eyes twinkling. "Well, two can play at that, young lady."

Christy pretended to swat at her friend with the makeshift broom. "You were pulling my leg the whole time."

" 'Course I was," Caney said, grinning now. "If you're set on stayin' here, then I will, too." She looked up at the deer hides sagging overhead. "We gonna live in this place, Miss Christy, we gotta put us some boards up there, and some tar paper, too, if we can get it. You have any of that money left? What you got for your mama's watch and pearls back in Richmond?"

Christy sank onto a bale of hay and sighed. "It took every penny to buy the mules and food and sign on with the wagon train. I'll take the cameo into town tomorrow. Surely some miner will want it for a present." Tears stung behind her eyes at the prospect of yet another stranger taking possession of one of Jenny's belongings, but she would not shed them. She had certainly had her differences with her mother, but she'd loved her. In spite of everything, the losses, the separations, the grim, unhappy days at St. Martha's, and the even unhappier visits to Fieldcrest, she'd loved her.

Caney's large, slender hand came to rest on Christy's shoulder. "Life'd be some easier for you if it weren't for that McQuarry pride of yours," she said quietly. "Now, let's gather some firewood and carry in the trunks from that wagon out there. We push some of these bales together, we can make us some beds. Better'n sleepin' under the wagon like we did whilst we was travelin'."

Christy laid her hand over Caney's, squeezed. "What's wrong with me, Caney?" she whispered. "Why can't I be beholden to Bridget or anybody else, even for something as basic as a real roof over my head?"

"I done told you already," Caney said. "It's that ole devil, pride. You got it from your granddaddy—he sure had him plenty, ole Mister Gideon McQuarry. Turns a body cussed, that's fo' sure. But it makes you strong, too. Keeps you goin' right on when other folks would lay down and whimper."

Christy blinked a few times, stood up, and went back to her sweeping. When that was done, she and

Caney brought in the trunks and pushed bales together to make three beds. There were plenty of quilts, hand-stitched by Rebecca McQuarry herself, and knitted woolen blankets, for Caney had rescued them from the laundry before she'd left the farm. They spread them over the prickly surfaces of the hay and made jokes about princesses and peas.

By the time Megan returned, accompanied by Skye, twilight was falling, and there was a cheerful blaze crackling in the middle of the lodge. The mules had been let out to pasture, along with horses borrowed from the army, their things had been brought in from the wagon, and Caney had a pot of beans, dried ones left over from the journey west, simmering on the fire.

Megan gleamed as though she'd been polished, and her bright red-gold hair caught the firelight. She and Skye were both barefoot, having waded across the stream, and carried their shoes by the laces. "I had a real bath," Megan said, as proudly as if she'd never taken one before. "I used hot water and store-bought soap, too, and I didn't even have to hurry in case it got cold, because Bridget kept filling up the tea kettle and warming it on the stove."

Christy, seated on yet another bale of hay, smiled and leaned forward to stir the beans with a wooden spoon. "Well, now. I'm sure you must be entirely too fine to keep company with the likes of Caney and me. I expect you'd rather spend the night with Skye."

Megan was clearly torn between a perfectly natural yearning for creature comforts—she had done without them for a long time, without a single complaint—and a strong devotion to her older sister, and it moved Christy deeply, seeing that. Forced her to look down at the fire for a moment and swallow hard.

"Bridget sent you a dried apple pie," Skye put in quickly, as if fearing the silence, and set a covered basket on the dirt floor, close to Christy's right foot. "She can't bake a decent cake to save her life, but she's got a way with pie dough."

Christy spoke carefully. Quietly. "Please tell her I said thank you," she told the girl gently, then shifted her gaze to Megan. "You go on across the creek with Skye, now. The two of you have been apart for a long time—you must have a lot of giggling to catch up on."

Megan looked doubtful, and at the same time full of hope. "You're sure?" Her voice was small. "You wouldn't mind?"

"I won't be alone, Megan," Christy pointed out tenderly. "I've got Caney to keep me company."

Megan hesitated just a moment longer, then bent and kissed Christy on the cheek. "I'll be back first thing in the morning," the girl promised earnestly. "You'll be needing a lot of help. Maybe I can catch us some fish for supper."

Christy reached out, patted her sister's hand. As children, Megan and Skye had been thicker than the proverbial thieves. She wasn't about to let her own problems with Bridget come between them. "That would be a fine thing," she said.

With that, the girls vanished into the night again, and their happy chatter trailed behind them like music.

"You did the right thing, lettin' that girl go like that. I know you worry about her whenever she's out of your sight," Caney observed, taking the spoon from Christy's hands and serving up a plate of beans for each of them.

"She'll be safe with Trace and Bridget," Christy said. Safer, certainly, than in an old Indian lodge with no door and no windows and only the flimsiest excuse for a roof.

The two women ate in companionable silence, both of them sick to death of boiled beans, and Caney insisted on carrying the dishes down to the creek for washing. When she returned, Christy had put on a nightgown, unpinned her waist-length hair, and begun to brush it with long, rhythmic strokes. She'd lit a kerosene lamp against the descending darkness and set the basket containing Bridget's pie inside one of the recently emptied trunks, in hopes of discouraging mice. It would be a fine treat for breakfast.

Caney undressed in the shadows and donned her own night dress, a fancy red taffeta affair trimmed in lace. It had been given to her by a sick woman she and Christy had tended while they were crossing the plains with the wagon train. The lady, one Lottie Benson, accompanied by a man she said was her brother, must certainly have had a story to tell, but Christy hadn't dared to ask her. Besides, it was kind of fun, just speculating.

"I reckon you know that good-lookin' marshal has an eye for you?" Caney asked, stretching out on her spiky bed with a long-suffering sigh.

The idea warmed Christy in a way no nightgown, taffeta or flannel, could have done. She blew out the lamp and lay down to take her night's rest. "Nonsense," she said. "You're imagining things."

Caney sighed again, a comfortable, settling-in sigh. "We'll see 'bout that," she replied. "We'll just see."

Chapter 2

Christy awakened early the following morning, while Caney was still snoring quietly on the other side of the fire. She dressed in haste, attended to a brief bit of business in the woods, and went down to the creek to wash her face and hands. Although there was smoke curling from both chimneys rising from Bridget's roof, she saw no other sign that anyone was up and about.

She returned to the lodge, brushed her hair and wound it into a loose knot at the back of her head, then brought the small velvet pouch containing her mother's jewelry from its hiding place in the false bottom of one of the trunks. She spilled the meager contents into one palm—the cameo brooch she meant to sell that very day, a pearl and diamond ring, a pair of sapphire ear bobs, and a garnet necklace.

A sob rose in her throat, but she did not make a sound. Nonetheless, the silent cry reverberated through her spirit and found its place there, among her dreams and wishes and private sorrows. She closed her hand around the jewels for a moment—they were only trinkets, really, and she should not let herself be sentimental about them—and then resolutely tucked everything back into the bag except the cameo. When the pouch was hidden again, she rose from her knees, slipped the brooch into her skirt pocket, and set about brewing the morning coffee.

Caney awakened with a stretch and a crow of exuberance. "Now, then," she said, "it's a brand new morning, praise be to God, and I'm here to see it and set my feet on the ground!"

Christy smiled. Whenever she got to railing against the fate that had brought her to this pass of destitution, Caney always said or did something that brought her around. Heaven knew, there were plenty of other women in the world in far worse straits than she was—women with no friends, no land, no jewelry to pawn. The brothels of the West were full of such unfortunates—and just the thought of them was enough to give Christy nightmares. "I have business in town," she said simply, fetching Bridget's pie from its place of protection in the cedar-lined trunk. "I'll see about lumber and tar paper for the roof."

Caney sat up, looking rumpled in her red taffeta nightgown. "I'd best go with you," she said.

Christy shook her head, averted her eyes. It was bad enough, practically begging for what they needed. The prospect of Caney or anyone else she cared about looking on was beyond endurance. "You stay here. There's plenty to keep you busy, and anyway, this is something I need to do alone."

Caney understood pride, and she nodded solemnly. "All right, then," she said with reluctance, and produced a small, familiar derringer from her ancient valise. Granddaddy had given it to her years before, Christy knew, so she could protect herself when she was away from home. "You take this along. Just in case."

Christy accepted the pistol, more at ease with it than she would have expected, and slipped it into her pocket alongside the brooch. She had never fired a gun and hoped she wouldn't be called upon to do so, that day or any other, but these were dangerous times, and a woman alone was unquestionably vulnerable.

"You gonna walk to town?" Caney wanted to know. "I could saddle up one of them army horses for you, quick as that." She snapped her fingers and, after pawing through a trunk, ferreted out a well-worn dress of yellow calico. "You run into some bad-tempered critter or a band of Injuns, you'll have a fightin' chance on horseback—"

"The marshal said it was two miles into Primrose Creek. That is hardly any distance at all. Besides, I need to stretch my legs."

Caney gave up, but she wasn't happy about it. "Well, you just better be back here afore noon, missy, or I'll come lookin' for you myself, you hear?"

"I hear," Christy said with a laugh. After a cup of coffee and a slice of Bridget's more than passable dried apple pie, she set out for town, following the rutted trail that passed for a road.

The countryside between the McQuarry land and

the town itself was forested, though not densely so, and Christy walked with her shoulders back, her head up, and her arms swinging, lest some cougar or mama bear catch sight of her and mistake her for easy prey. She imagined a highwayman or a hostile native behind every tree trunk and boulder, but she reached the edge of town after an estimated three-quarters of an hour, and stood at the foot of the main thoroughfare, taking it all in.

There were tents everywhere, and the noise of steam-powered saws clawed at her eardrums. She counted four saloons and several rustic storefronts, but as far as she could make out, there wasn't a single church or schoolhouse.

The road was rutted, though here and there an effort had been made to fill the potholes with small stones and sawdust, and she would have to be careful not to drag her hems through mud or step in a pile of horse manure. She lifted her chin and proceeded toward the mercantile, a two-story structure with a false facade and a distinct list to the lefthand side. The plank walls were chinked with a mixture of mud and plaster, and an enormous and exceedingly ugly black dog lay curled in front of the door.

Christy paused at the edge of the slanted board sidewalk and assessed the creature.

"He's just for show," a familiar voice put in from behind her. Marshal Zachary Shaw; she knew even before she turned to look at him. "Old Rufus there, he hasn't got a tooth in his head, nor a mean thought, either."

Skirts in hand, Christy schooled her expression to one of polite reserve. "Good morning, Marshal," she said, noting that he was freshly shaven and sporting clean clothes. His badge gleamed on the well-worn buckskin of his vest. She glanced at the dog—she should have guessed it was harmless, since it hadn't even troubled itself to bark at her—still snoozing on the doorstep. "How comforting to know you're around to keep us all safe."

He merely grinned at the mild jibe and hooked his thumbs in the front of his gun belt. It was just plain bad luck that he was so fine to look at, worse still that the pull she felt toward him was something as ancient as the stars. "You can count on me, ma'am."

She remembered the brooch in her pocket and her morning's mission. She had to get it over with, and quickly. Too much delay would only make matters worse. "If you'll excuse me—"

He nodded, and when she turned to head into the general store, intent upon speaking with the merchant, she collided with a man roughly as tall and substantial as a tree trunk. Looking up, she saw a square, handsome face, a head of curly brown hair, and a pair of concerned hazel eyes. His hands, big as stove lids, clasped her shoulders lest she fall.

"Are you all right?" he demanded. "Did I hurt you?"

Christy blinked, still a bit stunned.

"I don't reckon she'll have any scars to show for meeting you, Jake," Mr. Shaw put in. He had stepped onto the sidewalk now, and, disconcertingly, his presence had far more of an impact on Christy's senses than the close proximity of the man he'd called Jake. "Christy McQuarry, meet Jake Vigil. He owns Vigil Timber and Mining. Jake, Miss McQuarry."

"Mr. Vigil," Christy said, somewhat shyly.

The lumberman finally realized that he was still holding on to her shoulders and dropped his hands to his sides. He was dressed all in buckskins, Christy noted, and burly as an ox. Color throbbed in his neck and along his jawline. "Miss McQuarry," he said, and gulped.

"Jake here is a genuine timber baron," Zachary said easily.

Mr. Vigil shook his head, still blushing. Christy thought it was charming that such a strong man could be so modest, even retiring. "I reckon I'd better be getting back to the mill," he blurted, and, in his apparent confusion, he raised a hand to tip a nonexistent hat. Then, still red as a pepper, he fled, nearly stumbling over the dog, which had repositioned itself in the shade of the horse trough in front of the store.

Zachary watched his friend's retreat with a look of sympathetic amusement. For his own part, he was completely at ease, his hat pushed to the back of his head, one arm braced almost negligently against the post supporting the small roof that served as an awning above the door of the mercantile. "Poor Jake," he said. "He gets his feet tangled in his tongue whenever he runs across a pretty lady."

Christy ducked her head to hide a blush of her own and was irritated with herself for succumbing even that much to Mr. Shaw's rascally charms. "Unlike some men," she replied, "who always seem to have a glib remark waiting on the tip of their tongue."

He grinned, undaunted. "He's a rich man, Jake is. You see that mansion on the other side of the mill? That's his. Lives in it all by his lonesome."

Christy's heartbeat quickened, but at the same time, she felt a little sick to her stomach. Had she mentioned her plans to marry for security to Zachary Shaw at some point? She was certain she hadn't.

"Is that so?" she replied, bluffing. "And what makes you think I'm interested in the state of Mr. Vigil's bank account?"

He leaned close, spoke in a low voice meant to nettle. "Oh, I just guessed," he drawled. The nerve. "A plain woman can do real well for herself out here, Miss McQuarry. A beautiful one—like you—can name her price."

Christy wasn't sure whether she'd just been complimented or insulted—a little of both, she suspected, but mainly the latter. And she was riled. Hard put, in fact, not to give Zachary a tongue-lashing he'd never forget. "I do hope, Mr. Shaw, that you are not insinuating—"

He tugged his hat brim forward again so it shadowed his eyes. "I'm not insinuating anything. I'm saying it straight out. You could have any man in this town, and Jake Vigil would probably suit you just fine. He's got a big house and money, and he'll let you do all the talking, like as not." With that, the marshal of Primrose Creek thrust himself away from the support pole and strode away, leaving Christy to stare after him in frustration.

"I can help you, miss?"

Christy turned and saw a man as big as Mr. Vigil looming in the doorway. He was obviously the store's proprietor, for he wore a white apron over his shirt and trousers, a visor, and an air of genial authority.

"I am Gus," he said.

Christy had recovered enough to remember the reason for her errand by then, and she put out a hand, which Gus politely shook. She introduced herself and, at Gus's invitation, followed him inside. The interior of the store was rustic but clean and fairly well supplied for a frontier enterprise. The good, earthy smells of coffee beans, wood smoke, fresh sawdust, and new leather greeted her, and she breathed them in appreciatively.

It would have been wrong, though, to pretend that she was in a position to purchase anything of substance, so Christy approached the counter, several boards stretched between two giant barrels, and laid her mother's brooch in plain view.

"I have fallen upon difficult times, Mr.—er—Gus," she said forthrightly, keeping her spine very straight and her chin high. "I was hoping you might—perhaps—sell this for me, on consignment?" In the end, she couldn't bring herself to ask this kindly man to purchase the cameo outright.

Gus examined the piece carefully, frowning thoughtfully as he did so. "It is beautiful thing, no?"

"Yes," Christy agreed, and blinked.

"Miners and lumbermen, they all the time ask me for pretty things to give their womens. Perhaps I make a present to my sister, Bertha, to make her smile."

Tears burned behind Christy's eyes. Her mother had treasured that brooch, a gift from Christy and Megan's father on their wedding day, and she had worn it often. There were many, many memories attached to that piece and all the others. "It is very old. And very valuable."

Gus, still pondering the cameo, slapped down a meaty hand with such force that Christy jumped. "I buy," he said. "Fifty dollars."

Fifty dollars! It was a fortune, surely enough to put a real roof on the lodge, and maybe a door, too. "Th-thank you," Christy said, and turned crimson. She was wildly relieved, and at the same time, she felt as though she'd sold a part of herself along with the trinket.

Gus dropped the cameo into the pocket of his apron, then carefully counted out the agreed sum in coins of gold and silver. Christy thanked him again, scooped up the small fortune, and turned to make for the door, just in case he was inclined to change his mind.

"Miss," he called, just as she reached the threshold.

Christy's stomach dropped, and it was all she could do to turn around and meet the storekeeper's friendly gaze instead of running like a thief. "Yes?"

"You want Mama's pin back again, you come to Gus. He'll save it for you."

"But your sister—"

Gus shrugged massive shoulders. "Bertha is simple woman. She like plain things best."

Christy couldn't speak; it had been a long time since she had encountered such generosity. She nodded once, quickly, and dashed out the door, lest she break down and blather like a ninny. The black dog sat on its haunches on the sidewalk and gave a low, sorrowful whimper as she passed.

Five minutes later, she was standing in front of Jake Vigil's house, gaping. The white-clapboard structure was twice the size of the farmhouse back home, and it had gabled windows, each one boasting dark blue shutters, and a veranda that surrounded it like the deck railing of a Mississippi riverboat. A white picket fence enclosed it all, and there were fledgling rosebushes planted on either side of the stone steps.

After admiring the place as long as she dared, Christy turned and headed for the sawmill, where she had legitimate business. She intended to buy materials for a roof, and nobody, not even Zachary Shaw, could find fault with that. Not that she intended to give him the opportunity.

Jake Vigil greeted her with surprised pleasure. On his own ground, in the office of his thriving lumber business, he was far more at ease. He invited Christy to sit down and even offered her coffee, which she politely refused.

"I'm here to place an order," she announced. She had hated parting with her mother's brooch, even temporarily, but there was a certain exhilaration in achieving the purpose she had set for herself. "For a roof. I'll take tar paper, too, if you can get it."

Mr. Vigil perched on a corner of his large and cluttered desk, regarding her thoughtfully. "A roof?" No doubt, if he had recognized the name *McQuarry,* he'd assumed she was staying with Bridget and Trace.

"For the Indian lodge, out by Primrose Creek," she said, and squirmed only a little under his pensive gaze.

"The Indian lodge?"

Christy suppressed a sigh. Did the man echo *everything* that was said to him? Perhaps he was stupid—but how could that be? He'd built an empire, apparently under his own power. "My sister, Megan, and I are cousins to Mrs. Qualtrough and *her* sister, Skye. We inherited half the tract, specifically twelve hundred and fifty acres on this side of the stream. As Trace and Bridget already have a houseful, well, it seemed more prudent to restore the lodge as best we can and live there until other arrangements can be made."

She had to look away briefly when she uttered the last part.

"Jupiter's ghost," he marveled in a voice that would have shaken Mount Olympus itself. "You can't live in that—that hut!"

She leaned forward in her chair. She clasped her pride like a lifeline. "I assure you, Mr. Vigil, we can. And we shall, for the time being, at least."

He shook his head in frank amazement. "I'll be deuced," he said. "What does Trace have to say about this plan of yours?"

"A great deal, I'm sure," Christy replied, gathering her skirts and rising from her chair with as much grace and dignity as she could manage. "However, he is Bridget's husband, not mine, and I am under no constraints to obey him. Now, Mr. Vigil, will you or will you not sell me the materials I require for a roof?"

He muttered something, then nodded. "I'll have the things you need delivered first thing tomorrow morning."

"Thank you," Christy said with a brisk note in her voice. They agreed upon a price—one that fortunately left her with a few dollars to spare—and then she took her leave.

As she'd promised Caney, she was home before noon. Megan was down by the creek, fishing for supper, and from the looks of the mess of trout she held up for Christy to see, it would be a feast. Caney was a few yards downstream, beating laundry against a large, flat rock. Seeing Christy, they both smiled, and though Megan went right on fishing, Caney wrung out the petticoat she'd been washing, draped it over a bush, and plodded up the bank.

"Well?" she asked, without preamble.

"I got fifty dollars for it," Christy whispered. "And we'll have all the necessary supplies for our roof by tomorrow."

Caney narrowed her eyes and let her hands rest on her wide hips. "There's somethin' you ain't tellin' me, missy. Now, just what would that be?"

Christy drew a deep breath and let it out slowly.

"Today I met the man I'm going to marry," she said, and tried very hard to smile.

Two wagons, one loaded with timber and one with great rolls of tar paper, each rig drawn by four sturdy mules, rolled up to the lodge the next day around eight, when Christy, Caney, and Megan were all busy clearing ground for a garden. Although Trace had lent them the use of a plow and even harnessed one of the work horses to it, the labor was hard, and all three women were sweating and covered in dirt from head to foot.

Christy was alarmed when she recognized one of the drivers, for he was none other than Marshal Shaw. He looked her over, from tousled hair to muddy hem, and grinned. Driving the wagon beside his was a tall, powerfully built black man, a stranger who probably worked for Mr. Vigil. Several men on horseback rode in behind them.

"What are you doing here?" she demanded, swiping at a persistent fly. Out of the corner of her eye, she saw Caney and Megan exchange a glance.

"Just lending a hand wherever I can," Shaw answered smoothly. "This is Malcolm Hicks," he said, indicating his silent companion, who jumped down from the wagon seat, nodded once, and started pulling on a pair of heavy leather gloves. "He's the foreman over at the mill. I figured he could use some help unloading the wagons." The riders got down from their horses and left them to graze in the deep grass.

"Why don't you git down and help me, then,"

Hicks grumbled to Zachary, rounding the rig, lowering the tailgate, and grasping a stack of planks. " 'Stead of just settin' up there yammerin'."

Shaw grinned, secured the brake lever and the reins, and did as he was told. "Don't mind Malcolm," he whispered to Christy moments later as he passed too close, balancing three heavy boards on one shoulder. The four other men were busy, too. "He's not the sociable sort."

Christy said nothing. She wasn't going to give Zachary the pleasure of knowing he'd succeeded in throwing her off balance again. And she would have died before letting him so much as guess that just being near him made her heartbeat quicken and her breath turn shallow.

"You reckon he's married?" Caney inquired much later, when all the lumber was neatly stacked beside the lodge. A third wagon had arrived, filled with tools and kegs of nails and other bits and pieces, and the riders unloaded those things, too. Hicks and the marshal were supervising.

"Do you mean Mr. Hicks?" Christy asked distractedly, wiping the back of her neck with a wadded sunbonnet. She was tired, hot, and almost desperate enough to swallow her pride and ask Bridget if she could make use of her bathtub, just this once.

"*Yes,* I mean Mr. Hicks," Caney retorted impatiently. "It's a cinch I ain't sweet on the marshal, fetchin' though he is. I'm old enough to be his mama. 'Sides, I like my men dark-skinned and serious."

Christy sighed. Mr. Hicks certainly met Caney's

requirements on both counts. Except for the remark he'd made to Zachary about helping to unload the lumber, he hadn't said a single word the whole time he was there, nor had he spared so much as a smile for any of them. "For heaven's sake," she said. "You don't even know the man. He could be a fiend."

Caney was still watching Mr. Hicks in a most frank and forward fashion. "I know all I needs to, 'cept for one thing—if'n he's got him a wife—and I mean to find that out right quick."

"How?"

"I'm goin' over the creek and ask Bridget, that's how," Caney replied. Then she brushed her hands against her skirts, adjusted the old floppy brimmed hat she wore to keep the sun off her head, and set herself for the Qualtrough place.

Megan had gone back to picking rocks out of the garden plot and carrying them to the growing pile beside the lodge's southern wall, and Skye and Noah had come to help. At the rate the three of them were going, they'd have enough stones for a fireplace every bit as grand as Bridget's before sunset, even if they *were* prattling the whole time.

Megan had always had exceptional hearing, and she was something of an eavesdropper, too, despite all her sterling qualities. Straightening, hands resting on her slender hips, she smiled. "Wouldn't that be something," she said, "if our Caney got herself another husband!"

Christy blew out a long breath, causing tendrils of sweat-dampened hair to dance against her forehead.

Then, without answering, she marched over, took up the reins again, and urged the plow horse back into motion.

By nightfall, she was so dirty that she feared her skin would never be the same, her feet and legs were aching, and her palms were covered with raw blisters. She'd barely touched her supper—a batch of fried chicken Bridget had kindly sent over in Skye's keeping—and she wanted nothing so much as to fold her arms, drop her head, and sob. She was too tired to bother with a bath, and too miserable not to, and when it came right down to it, she just couldn't bring herself to ask her cousin for anything more. It was galling enough that Bridget felt she had to provide meals for her indigent relations. She was probably over there in that warm, tidy house of hers, shaking her head and clucking her tongue. *That Christy,* she would be saying to Trace. *She's as stubborn as ever.*

Unable to bear the thought of going to bed in her present state, however, Christy gathered her nightgown, an old flour sack that served as a towel, and a bar of scented soap Skye had given Megan as a gift. She made her way down to the creek, found a place sheltered by trees and bushes, and stripped to the skin.

The water was bone-jarringly cold, but it numbed the soreness in Christy's muscles and soothed the insect bites covering her legs and arms. She washed her hair thoroughly, knowing it would be a trial to brush when she got back to the lodge, then bathed the rest of her body. She was about to brave the chilly air of an April night when she saw a bobbing lantern light and heard a rustling in the brush.

"Who's there?" she called. She tried to speak with authority, but she knew she lacked conviction.

"Don't fret," Megan replied, flailing through the greenery to plop down gratefully on a rock. "It's only me. Are you trying to catch pneumonia? This creek is fed by melting snow!" She tossed Christy the flour-sack towel and lowered her eyes while her sister got out of the water to dry off and put her nightgown on.

Christy's teeth were chattering. "I'm f-fine," she said.

Megan sighed. "You're not fine," she replied. "You've run yourself ragged. Caney and I agree that you need to let up a little. Rest. Read. Go out riding like you used to do at home. Christy, I can't remember the last time I saw you smile—*really* smile, I mean."

Christy sighed. "I'll do those things when the work is done," she said.

Megan frowned, and a bit of her redhead's temper showed in her eyes, even in the unsteady light of the lamp. "I know what you're planning, Christy," she said, "and I'll have no part of it. I will not see my only sister work herself into an early grave on my account."

"Who says it's on your account?" Christy asked, but her voice was a little shaky. Bluffs didn't always work with Megan. "I'd like to live in a grand house, wear lovely clothes—"

"Which is why you've set your cap for Jake Vigil?"

"Who told you that?"

"Never mind who told me. Just don't throw your life away on my account. I'll never forgive you if you do."

"But your wonderful mind, Megan. College and travel and fine things—"

"Are you sure those aren't *your* dreams, Christy?" Megan interrupted. "Because they certainly aren't mine!"

Christy was dumbfounded and not a little wounded.

Megan was already turning to go off and leave her. "I'm getting married and having babies," she said. "That's what I want. A husband and a house and babies." With that, she was gone.

Christy dressed slowly and made her own way up the hillside, her footsteps guided by the light of the moon. When she reached the place that would be home, at least until she managed to marry Mr. Vigil, she found that Megan had already gone to bed. If she wasn't sound asleep, she pretended to be.

Caney was sitting by the fire, sipping a last cup of coffee and reflecting.

"Mr. Malcolm Hicks had himself a wife once," she said, without looking at Christy. "Her name was Polly, and she died of the consumption three years ago."

Christy found her comb and began working the tangles out of her wet hair. She was so tired she thought sure she could have fallen asleep on her feet, like an old horse in a field, and the echo of her conversation with Megan down by the creek bounced painfully through her mind and heart. "Well, you certainly didn't waste any time finding out what you wanted to know."

"I never do," Caney replied, and pressed a plug of tobacco inside one cheek. "I figured on asking Bridget, but she was feeling poorly—mind you, that girl is carryin' twins, no matter what everybody else says—so I hunted up Trace. He claims the whole town thinks highly of Mr. Hicks."

Christy struggled patiently with a snarl in her hair, biting her lip against the pain. "Lord have mercy," she teased. "Lord have mercy on us all."

Zachary made his rounds, arrested a pair of drunken cowboys to keep them from shooting up the town, and locked them in the small enclosed room that served as the jailhouse's only cell. Untroubled by their descent into shame and degradation, they decided to sing and set every dog in Primrose Creek to howling in accompaniment. Coupled with the racket coming from the saloons, it was hardly noticeable.

He poured himself a cup of coffee, considered adding a shot of whiskey, and decided against it. A couple of drinks, and he'd be singing along with his prisoners.

He set the cup down on a corner of his desk, loosened the strand of rawhide that secured his holster to his thigh, unbuckled his gun belt, and hung the whole works on a peg within easy reach of his chair. Miss Nelly would be upset if he didn't turn up before she blew out the lamps and put the cat out; she wanted all her regular boarders present and accounted for, but he didn't like leaving the singing cowboys unguarded.

He wasn't worried that they'd escape—they were both so drunk that neither of them could have covered his ass with a ten-gallon hat—but Primrose Creek was a canvas and dry-wood town, cheroots were popular, and fire was a very real threat. He couldn't risk letting his guests roast like a couple of stuffed pigs, which meant he'd have to sleep in his chair.

Not, he thought with a low chuckle, that he was likely to do that. He hadn't slept a whole night through since he met Miss McQuarry, and the problem showed no signs of abating. He was a damn fool, that's what, contriving ways to meet up with her when she'd already made it plain that she wanted a life wholly different from anything he could have given her. It would have been safer, not to mention smarter, to drag a couple of sticks of flaming firewood out of the stove and juggle them.

He blew out the lamp on his desk, sat back in his chair, and put his feet up, resting the heels of his worn boots on a copy of the *Territorial Enterprise,* published down in Virginia City. She'd looked a sight that morning when he and Hicks and the others had delivered the lumber, he thought with an involuntary grin, cupping his hands behind his head. From the state of her dress, she might have caught fire and rolled on the ground to put herself out, and her hair had been filled with grass and plain old dirt and falling around her shoulders in loops. For a long moment, he hadn't been able to catch his breath, might have been sitting there in that wagon box still, staring like a dumbfounded fool, if Malcolm hadn't broken the spell by inviting him to help unload the lumber.

He sighed and closed his eyes as the cowboys launched into a sentimental piece about long-suffering mothers watching at the parlor window for their "darling boy" to come marching home from war. They were way off key, the fellows were, but the dogs were doing all right.

She's going to marry Jake Vigil and his sawmill and his big house, he told himself silently, and it didn't do any good at all, even though he knew every word was true. He'd better find a way to put her out of his mind, and soon, or he'd go crazy.

One of the songsters began to pound at the heavy wooden door of the cell. "Marshal!" he yelled. "Hey, Marshal, you out there?"

"*What?*" Zachary shouted back.

"Can't somebody shut up them damn dogs?"

Zachary laughed. Whatever happened with Miss McQuarry, he would still have the singular joys of his work.

Chapter 3

When Jake Vigil came to help put up the roof, he brought a crew of more than a dozen men along, and a handful of yellow and blue wildflowers to boot. While his workers swarmed over the lodge like bees on a piece of fallen fruit, Mr. Vigil approached Christy, his face flaming.

"These are for you," he said. "I reckon you know my intentions."

Christy was charmed, but at the same time, she felt a distinct stab of conscience. While marrying the timber baron would certainly serve many purposes, Jake certainly deserved a wife who genuinely loved him. She'd not felt any particular stirrings, the few times she'd seen him, and she feared she never would, no matter how long she lived or how kind and generous he might be or how many children she bore him. Megan's heated words of the night before beside the creek roared in her ears. *Are you sure these aren't your dreams, Christy? I'm getting married and having babies . . . that's what I want.*

Well, she thought resolutely, Megan didn't know what she was throwing away, that was all. It was up to her, Christy, to behave in everyone's best interests.

Everyone's except Jake Vigil's, possibly.

Just then, catching a glimpse of a cocoa-colored stallion at the edge of the small clearing, she feared she would never be able to put Marshal Zachary Shaw's irritating personage completely out of her mind. So far, her efforts had certainly been unsuccessful.

"Mornin', Miss McQuarry," he said, as if drawn to her side by the power of her thoughts, catching the brim of his hat lightly and briefly between thumb and forefinger. He nodded to Mr. Vigil, who was still standing rooted to the grass, the mass of flowers beginning to faint in his large hand. "Jake."

Jake returned the nod, but he didn't look entirely pleased to see Zachary. "I reckon things must be pretty peaceful in town, Marshal, if you've got the time to come out here and socialize."

Christy's hand shook a little as she reached out to rescue the blossoms from Jake's fist. "I'll just put these in water," she said, and turned in haste toward the lodge.

Jake caught her arm in a gentle grasp, however, and stopped her. He cleared his throat and colored up again. "I'm holding a party over at my place on Saturday night. To welcome you and the other ladies to Primrose Creek. I hope you'll come."

Zachary was watching her closely and with benign interest. She did her best to ignore him, but it was difficult, as usual. If she'd been the least bit superstitious, she would have thought he'd cast a spell over her.

She kept her gaze trained on Jake's face. She would wear one of her mother's fancy ball gowns, she told herself, and make the most of the opportunity—and to the devil with Zachary Shaw. "I'm flattered, Mr. Vigil. Certainly, we'll be there." With that, she spun around and dashed, flowers in hand, toward the shadowy doorway of the lodge.

Using an enamel cup for a vase, Christy placed the bluebells and buttercups in the last of the drinking water and hoisted the bucket, with its familiar tin ladle. After filling the pail again at the edge of the creek, she carried it back up and set it on the tailgate of one of Mr. Vigil's wagons.

Already, Zachary and Mr. Hicks were measuring off a large log to be used as the center beam, while others set up sawhorses and began cutting thick planks of ponderosa pine to equal lengths. Trace arrived shortly, pushed up his sleeves, and joined in the work. Bridget came along, though she settled herself, at her husband's insistence, on a large, moss-covered stone in the shade. She looked bulky and overheated in her advanced state of pregnancy, but her smile was as serene as that of a Renaissance madonna, and joy glowed from within her, lucent and pure.

Christy watched her cousin for a long moment, full of wonder and no little envy—this, then, was how a woman looked when she bore the children of a man she truly loved—but quickly regained control of her emotions. She'd made her choice, to marry for sensible reasons, hoping that love and passion would come later, and practicality demanded that she stand by the decision. There was no use whatsoever in bemoaning any of the sacrifices; better to concentrate on the rewards. Better to remember how it was, first at that wretched school in England and then in Virginia, when they found everything changed and those Yankees living in Granddaddy's house. Her desolation had been complete, and though she believed she had hidden her fears from Megan, Caney had certainly understood. It had been Caney gave them cots in her tiny shack of a house, Caney who fed them, Caney who suggested traveling west, taking up the bequest, and starting over fresh.

What would she have done without Caney? Shaking her head, Christy filled a clean cup from the ladle in the water bucket and carried it across the deep grass to where Bridget was sitting. "Sorry," she said with a small but sincere smile. "I haven't the makings for a proper cup of tea."

Bridget accepted the water with a grateful nod, taking the mug in both hands. "Thanks," she said. She inclined her head toward the lodge, surrounded by busy builders. The sounds of hammers and saws rose on the soft spring air. "Looks as though you'll have a proper roof by mid-afternoon," she commented, and made room for Christy to sit down beside her.

The rock was hard, and Christy squirmed a little, trying in vain to make herself comfortable.

Bridget's McQuarry-blue eyes were full of friendly

amusement. "You might want to sit in the grass instead," she said. "It's softer. After all, I've got padding."

Christy laughed, searched Megan out in the crowd, and saw her sister handing nails to a good-looking young scoundrel with dark hair and a mischievous grin. Some of her pleasure in the day ebbed.

Bridget must have followed her gaze. "That's Caleb Strand," she said. "He's nice, hardworking, and entirely harmless."

Christy sighed. Young Mr. Strand might be all those things, but she meant to keep an eye on him all the same. She knew what was good for Megan, and marriage to a lumberjack was not on the list. No, Megan would go to school, perhaps in San Francisco or Denver, when the necessary funds became available. Eventually, she would marry a man she loved, but one from a substantial family, and never lack for so much as a hairpin for as long as she lived.

"Megan," she said at last, "will not be staying on at Primrose Creek. Not for long, in any event."

Bridget looked surprised. "Whyever not? This is her home now, as well as yours."

No, Bridget, Christy wanted to say, *this is* your *home. I will always be your cousin, who came from far away.*

"There is nothing here for Megan," she said firmly, just as Zachary caught her eye again. Even though he wasn't looking at her, she couldn't seem to look away. "As beautiful as this place is, it's—well—remote."

Bridget bristled almost imperceptibly. "Don't you mean backward?"

"I didn't say that!" Christy protested. Zachary had set aside his hat or lost it somewhere, and his hair gleamed in the sunlight like spun gold. Even from that distance, she was struck in the midsection by the pure visceral impact of his grin, flashing white in his tanned face. At last, she managed to look away and met Bridget's gaze again. "Even you have to admit that Primrose Creek is hardly the place for a polished young lady."

Bridget rolled her eyes. "Jupiter's ghost, but you are impossible."

Christy sat up a little straighter and spoke just as one of the workmen came into range, looking for the bucket of drinking water with its community ladle. "I've seen the 'town' of Primrose Creek for myself, Bridget, and it's no fit habitation for anything but men and mules!"

The worker paused, gave Christy an indignant look, and walked away without touching the ladle.

Bridget hissed like water spilling from the spout of a kettle onto a hot stove. "Do you *want* people to dislike you, Christy—is that it? That way, you don't have to take the risk of caring for somebody, right?"

Christy felt a surge of temperament move through her, but she kept a tight hold on her composure. She studied her fingers, which were tightly interlaced. "What would you suggest I do? Marry my sister off to the highest bidder, just to prove I don't think she's too good for these—these people?"

"Why not?" Bridget asked in a sharp whisper. "Isn't that what you plan to do with your own life? Marry yourself off to the highest bidder?"

Christy was at once stricken and furious. It must have been a moment of weakness that made her blurt out her private thoughts to Bridget that first day at Primrose Creek, and now, of course, she wished she'd held her tongue. "My plans," she said, when she dared speak, "are my own business, Bridget Qualtrough, and I will thank you to tend to your knitting."

Some of the starch seemed to go out of Bridget; she wilted a little, as the thirsty wildflowers had done earlier. Cupping her chin in one hand, she sighed heavily. "There we go, bickering again," she lamented. Her eyes were clear when she caught Christy's gaze and held it. "I just want you to be happy, that's all."

Christy's throat thickened. No one, she realized, had ever said that to her, save her beloved Granddaddy, of course. She swallowed painfully. "Different things please different people," she said at great length.

Bridget grasped her hand, squeezed it. "Christy, listen to me—"

But Christy could not afford to listen, to fall prey to a lot of romantic dreams. Her life was not like her cousin's, never had been and never would be. She shot to her feet and pulled her hand from Bridget's. "You have Trace," she said, watching as Bridget's son chased a butterfly through the high grass nearby, and Skye, in turn, chased him. "You have little Noah, and a new baby coming, and a fine house to live in. What could you possibly know about my situation?"

"Christy, I was *in* your situation. I was just as stubborn and just as proud. Just as foolish. That's how I know you'll be making a terrible mistake if you marry anyone for any reason but love." She paused, no doubt aware that her words, unwanted as they were, were sinking in. "It wouldn't be fair to Jake, either," she added, granting no quarter. "He's a good man, Christy, and he deserves a woman who wants him for himself."

"I'm sure I would grow quite fond of him over the years," Christy allowed, raising her chin and folding her arms. She would never give Jake Vigil cause to regret taking her for a wife. Not willingly, at least. She would cook and sew and clean and—well, better to think about the rest another time.

"Fond?" Bridget challenged in a taut whisper. "You're going to be sharing his life. His bed. And believe me, *fond*ness will be small comfort—"

Christy put her hands over her ears. "Stop."

But Bridget went right on. "Have you ever experienced passion, Christy? Have you ever thought you'd lose your mind over a certain man's kisses and caresses?"

"Stop." Christy was pleading by then. She had dreamed of just such kisses and caresses, it was true, but lately in her imaginings, the man holding her in his arms was Zachary Shaw.

"I won't," Bridget persisted. "What I've found with Trace—when we're alone together, I mean—is, well, it's magical. It's intoxicating. I never imagined—" She blushed. "I married Mitch McQuarry because I liked him so much, because I thought somehow having a wife and family might keep him home from the war. What I'm trying to say is, it wasn't like that with

Mitch. It was tender. It was *fond*. And now that I understand what love—real love—between a man and a woman can mean—"

Christy looked away, still hugging herself, nearer tears than ever. She was innocent of any man's touch, fond or otherwise, but she grasped what Bridget was saying only too well. "I'd better send Megan to the creek for more water," she said, out of pure desperation. "The men will be needing lots of it, I think, working so hard in this heat."

"You're not going to listen, are you?" Bridget's voice was quiet. Angrily resigned. "You're just going to go charging right ahead and ruin not only your own life but Jake's, too. And probably Megan's for good measure. Well, don't come crying to me when you're trapped in a loveless marriage and wanting Zachary every day and every night until the day you die."

Christy stared at her cousin. "How—what—?"

"How did I know you were sweet on Zachary? I've got eyes in my head, Christy. I saw the way you look at him. And, I might add, I saw the way he looks at you."

Christy's traitorous and undisciplined heart skipped over a beat and landed, skidding, upon the next. She could not keep herself from searching Zachary out with her eyes, finding him. Sure enough, he was watching her. Standing stock still, with his hands on his hips and his blond hair shining and his expression solemn. Even sad.

"I'd best get home," Bridget said, rising with some

difficulty from her perch on the mossy rock. "Noah is probably running wild, and poor Skye is so smitten with the little stinker, she'll be letting him get away with murder." She paused. "Think about what I said, Christy," she warned. "*Think* about it."

Christy did not answer. Couldn't answer. It was as though she and Zachary were linked by some fierce and fiery current; although well out of earshot, and certainly beyond his reach, he might have been touching Christy. Might have been caressing her cheeks with the sides of his thumbs, getting ready to kiss her—

With a violent effort, she wrenched her gaze free of his and turned away, bent on fetching more water, having completely forgotten that she'd meant for Megan to do that chore.

Dear God, Zachary wondered, why did he keep letting himself in for the kind of trouble a woman like Christy McQuarry could stir up? If he didn't stay away from her, he was bound to do something downright stupid, like haul her into his arms and kiss her so she stayed kissed. She'd probably shoot him for it, once she recovered, but it would almost be worth it.

He rubbed the back of his neck once, before turning to his work again. In the process, of course, he'd lose one of the best friends he had—Jake Vigil. For Jake was plainly just as taken with Miss McQuarry as he was.

For the remainder of that long, long day, he steered clear of Christy, working on top of the roof, once the joists and ridgepole had been lifted into place, on the strength of muttered curses, mules, steel cable, and a pulley the size of a wagon wheel, pounding nails with more force than the task required.

In the end, it was all for nothing, though, because when he climbed down the ladder, aching in every joint and longing for a hot bath and a double shot of whiskey, she was standing right there, with a ladle of water in one hand and fathoms of sorrow in her gray eyes. Without speaking, she handed him the ladle, and he took it and drank.

He nodded his thanks, and they just stood there, staring at each other, for a long time. And suddenly, he realized just how deep it went, what he felt for her. How it had taken root in his very soul.

"Mr. Shaw—I—"

He waited; he wanted to hear what she had to say, and, besides that, he was so shaken by his own realization that he didn't trust himself not to trip over his own tongue if he opened his mouth.

Her cheeks turned a delicious shade of apricot, and her eyes were the color of a cloudy sky. "I just wanted to tell you that—well—there's a whole pig cooking over at Bridget and Trace's place." She paused and flushed again, plainly at a loss. He wanted to grin, didn't dare. "There's going to be an outdoor supper. For everybody who helped with the roof."

He nodded, waited. A gentleman would probably have gotten her off the proverbial hook, but he was no gentleman and had never pretended to be.

"You're invited." She didn't look all that pleased and added reluctantly, "Same as everybody else."

He chuckled, thrust one hand through his hair, which was full of sweat and sawdust. "Well, now," he said, surprising himself that he could speak at all, let alone in a slow drawl, "I guess I've had more enthusiastic invitations in my time, but I do favor roasted pork, and I am about as hungry as I've ever been." He sketched a slight bow, one that would never pass muster in the gracious drawing rooms and parlors of the fancy folks back east and in England. "Thank you, Miss McQuarry. I'll be honored to attend."

She turned on one heel, without so much as a parting word, and walked away.

Damnation, he thought, enjoying the sway of her rounded hips and the fire of a dying sun in her ebony-dark hair. Here he'd made himself a sensible plan—to stay away from Christy—and as soon as he found himself face-to-face with her, he turned witless as a post. As for that other part, the part that would have him on one knee proposing marriage, well, it showed no signs of waning.

He was still watching her and pondering his own contradictory and misguided nature, when a hearty slap on the shoulder snapped him out of his reverie.

Jake Vigil laughed, a sound that had been known to set boulders rolling downhill, but there wasn't a whole lot of humor in his face. In fact, his usually friendly eyes were cold as high-country creek water in January. "Looks like you and I have taken a shine to the same filly, my friend," he said.

Zachary almost conceded the match, then and there, for he knew he'd been dealt a losing hand when it came to Christy McQuarry, but there was something inside him that wouldn't stand still for that. He'd lost one woman, one he'd loved very much. He hadn't had a chance then, but this time he did, however slim. However fleetingly, he'd known when he looked into Christy's eyes that she was drawn to him. "Looks like it," he agreed grimly. "I don't mind saying I wish things were different, though."

Jake's gaze was following Christy as she went to each of the workmen, shook his hand, and extended smiling thanks. It made Zachary's gut clench, seeing her smile like that at anybody who wasn't him; he felt like a buck in springtime, looking for a fight.

"You'll find yourself a wife in time," Jake said, and his tone was not without sympathy. The West was a lonely place, and the companionship of a good woman was no small consideration. A beautiful, intelligent, and spirited one, like Christy, was of infinite worth. "I mean to have Miss McQuarry there gracing my front parlor before the first snow."

Zachary had a few thoughts along that line himself—places Christy might grace—and none of them had to do with a parlor. Not that he had one, living at Miss Nelly's the way he did. He put out a hand to his friend. "I wish you the best of luck," he said.

Jake frowned, shaking Zachary's hand in a distracted way. "But you don't mean to back down, do you?"

Zach grinned. "I'm sorry. That's something I never really got the knack of doing."

Jake's responding grin was genuine if a little slippery. "Me, either," he said. "Now, I believe I'm going to have myself some of that roast pig over at the Qualtroughs' place."

Zachary retrieved his hat from the low branch where he'd left it and settled it on his head. "Sounds good," he answered.

After everyone had eaten all the pork they could hold, seated around the big bonfire in front of Bridget and Trace's house, Malcolm Hicks brought out a fiddle and began to play. Christy had never seen such a transformation in a man. Dour and silent before, Mr. Hicks became animated the instant he lifted his bow; his teeth flashed in a brilliant smile, and his eyes danced with enjoyment.

Soon another man joined in, pulling a harmonica from his shirt pocket. Members of the gathered crowd, tired from their hard work and sated by a delicious meal, clapped in time and tapped their feet. Trace swept a laughing Caney into his arms and waltzed her once, twice, around the fire, double-time. Then Megan whirled by, beaming, with young Caleb. Christy took a step forward, only to find herself whisked into the embrace of Zachary Shaw, going for a dizzying spin.

She felt as if she'd taken a particularly bad spill from a horse; there was no breath at all in her lungs, and she was a little dazed into the bargain. She hadn't the sense to protest and wasn't sure she would have done so, even if she'd been able.

In a moment, they were outside the rim of firelight, in the darkness, and the sounds of the party seemed to come from far, far away. Without any warning whatsoever, Zachary pulled Christy against him, bent his head, and kissed her. She squirmed at first, but then she was lost, returning the kiss, responding shamelessly, body and soul.

Finally, he set her away from him, though his hands remained on her upper arms. "That's all I wanted to know," he said. Then, hoarsely, "Christy?"

She drew a deep breath in an attempt to steady herself, but she was hopelessly adrift. The kiss, like the dance, had sent her spinning. "Y-yes?"

"Remember that." Then, as though he hadn't behaved badly enough already, he kissed her again, as soundly as before and at greater length. "And that," he said, gasping a little, when it was over. Then he simply walked away, leaving her standing there in the tall grass, every part of her still pulsing with a desire that would never be fulfilled. And at last, at long, long last, Christy McQuarry broke down and cried.

"It's good to have a proper roof over our heads again, at least," Caney remarked that night, when she and Christy and Megan had returned to the lodge. They all regarded their hay bale beds without enthusiasm, though, and Christy couldn't help remembering crisp linen sheets and feather mattresses and plump pillows. The fire burned low, flinging shadows onto the log walls of the lodge, and, far away, a coyote called a plaintive song to the moon.

"Umm," said Christy, who did not want to talk. Her eyes were still puffy, despite all the icy creek water she'd splashed onto her face, and she was afraid something in her voice would betray her feelings if she said too much. She undressed as far as her bloomers and camisole and laid herself down with a sigh.

"We got a door, too," Caney went on. "Fancy that. Up to now, an Injun or an old bear could have walked right in here and said how-dya-do."

"Um-hmm," Christy replied.

Megan, too, had gotten hastily into bed, and within a few moments, she was snoring delicately, all danced out.

"He'll make you a fine husband."

If Caney didn't get an answer of some sort, she'd just go right on chattering, half the night. "Jake?" Christy asked sleepily.

"Zachary," Caney said with surety.

Christy's eyes flew open. "Nonsense. You know how I feel about him."

"Exactly," came the satisfied response. "I saw you go off in the dark with that marshal. So did most everybody else, I reckon. Did he steal a kiss?"

Two, Christy thought, reliving them both in the space of a moment and fairly melting in the heat. *That's all I wanted to know,* he'd said.

"Of course not," she lied.

Caney chuckled. "Well, he might as well have, 'cause everybody thinks he did. Jake Vigil was fit to bite nails in half, and there were a few other unhappy fellers in the crowd, too."

Christy's face flamed in the darkness. It was mortifying to imagine the others gossiping about her, even though the rumors were true. And if she'd ruined her chances with Mr. Vigil, she would never forgive herself.

Saturday took its sweet time coming, but it finally arrived, and Christy was ready for the party long before it was time to leave for town. Caney and Megan had fussed all afternoon with her hair, and she'd taken in her mother's yellow silk, the French design with the daring neckline and sumptuous lace, so that it fit her perfectly, showing her figure off to best advantage. Caney was wearing her "church dress," a black bombazine, its austerity partially relieved by a modest pendant her late husband, Titus, had given her. Megan, with her auburn hair, ivory skin, and meadow-green eyes, looked like a visiting angel or a wood nymph in her gown of lightweight wine-colored velvet, also salvaged from Jenny's wardrobe.

"Skye and I have been *perishing* to see the inside of Mr. Vigil's house!" Megan confided, flushed with excitement at the prospect of a social evening. It had been a long time since either she or Christy had attended any sort of dress-up affair. "It looks so grand from the outside."

"Don't it, now?" Caney ruminated, but she was watching Christy as she spoke, not Megan. "I reckon the bed's mighty cold of a night, though, if there's no love there to fill it."

Christy glared.

"What?" Megan asked. Bless her heart, she was genuinely puzzled. When she got no reply, she prattled on. "Skye's madly in love with Mr. Vigil. I'm not supposed to tell, but there it is, I told."

"I reckon that'll pass," Caney said, "and Miss Skye will find somebody else entirely." Her tone was firm, and her gaze, still fixed on Christy, did not so much as flicker. " 'Fact, why don't you go and see if Trace is about ready with that wagon, Miss Megan. I don't fancy walkin' to town, party or no party."

Megan glanced at Christy, then pulled a shawl over her shoulders and went outside to watch for Trace and Bridget, Skye, and little Noah.

"If you're about to preach to me, Caney Blue," Christy warned in a whisper, "you'd do well to think better of it. I have had this argument with Bridget, and I *will not* have it with you."

Caney was a model of exasperated disgust. "You're a stiff-necked McQuarry, that's what you are."

"We've already established that."

Caney shook a finger. "Don't you smart-mouth me, young lady. You don't choose to argue, that's just fine with me. But you ain't got no choice but to listen!"

Just when the woman would have launched into a loud and colorful, not to mention familiar, sermon, arms waving for emphasis, they heard the unmistakable sounds of a team and wagon, and Megan burst through the door, eyes shining with eager excitement. "They're here!" she cried.

Christy hoped her sister's lively state of mind had nothing to do with Mr. Caleb Strand, though she suspected he was indeed the reason for Megan's special, sparkling prettiness. "Thank heaven," Christy said in the face of Caney's scowl.

"You don't need to think this discussion is over, miss," that good woman warned forcefully, " 'cause it ain't."

Christy donned her own shawl, a gossamer affair of filmy antique lace, made for beauty rather than warmth. She picked up the lantern and started for the door. "Let's not keep the Qualtroughs waiting," she said cheerfully.

The bed of the wagon was spacious and padded with fresh straw. Skye and Noah were already seated amid the spiky gold, smiling at the prospect of an evening of fun. Bridget was beside Trace in the box, and once again Christy noticed a glow about her cousin, as though she'd swallowed the moon whole.

Trace greeted the three women with a grin and a tilt of his hat, then climbed down from the wagon seat to help them aboard. Bridget held the reins competently while he lifted first Caney, then Megan, and finally Christy herself up into the fragrant straw. Noah scrambled up on his own. "We're going to be late!" he crowed.

"My goodness," Christy said, finding a place near Skye in the center of the wagon bed, "we'll be half an hour picking the hay from our hair."

Bridget chuckled but offered no comment. Caney and Megan settled themselves at the edge of the tailgate, which Trace had left suspended from its hinges, their limbs dangling over the ground.

"I reckon Mr. Hicks is goin' to be there," Caney said, making no effort whatsoever to hide her infatuation with a man she barely knew. She was going to get herself a reputation if she didn't take care.

Aren't you a fine one to talk, Christy scolded herself. *Heart all aflutter for one man and planning to marry another.* "Who will we see at this party?" she asked aloud.

"Everybody," Skye answered. She looked very grown-up in her pale blue taffeta dress. Her hair was pinned into a loose knot at the back of her head, and her dark brown eyes gleamed with delight. Christy wondered if her young cousin really was infatuated with Mr. Vigil and if she'd be hurt when he married.

"Including Zachary Shaw, I reckon," Caney put in, unsolicited.

Christy ignored her, or tried to, anyway. Caney Blue was not an easy woman to overlook, even in the best of circumstances. When she was determined to be heard, she was impossible.

"It's true that everyone will be there," Bridget put in, as Trace, beside her again, took up the reins and released the brake lever. "Out here, when there's a party, it's just assumed that all and sundry are welcome. You might see anyone from the governor to a fancy woman from the Golden Garter or Diamond Lil's."

Within a half hour, their way illumined by moonlight, the Qualtrough wagon took its place among a dozen others in front of Jake Vigil's magnificent house. Even in Virginia, the structure would have roused comment, with its leaded windows, sweeping veranda, and towering front door. Light gleamed through spotless glass, and the sounds of merriment and plenty spilled out into the night.

Christy drew a deep breath and let it out slowly, trying to collect herself. In truth, however, Caney's earlier comment echoed in her mind. *I reckon that bed's mighty cold of a night, if there's no love to fill it.*

Love, she scoffed, gathering her skirts after Trace had helped her down from the wagon. It was a fickle emotion, at best, dispensed by whimsical gods to the favored few. And what good had it done her mother, loving two men, both of whom had betrayed her in one way or another? No, indeed, there was no sense at all in placing too great a store by something so fragile and so fleeting.

Head high, shoulders squared, Christy walked resolutely toward the light and music. Toward the shining future that she had imagined for herself and for Megan, long ago, during those first terrible nights at St. Martha's school and many, many times since.

The inside of the house was beyond grand, with its gilded moldings, marble fireplaces, costly furniture, and mirrors fit to rival Versailles. Crystal chandeliers shimmered overhead, the flames of their candles flickering magically in every draft.

Jake Vigil greeted each of his guests personally, not excluding Christy, and it seemed he held her hand just a little longer than he had Bridget's. His hazel eyes held a quality of wonder, as though he saw only her and hadn't even noticed the grandeur around him.

The music was provided by Mr. Hicks and several friends, and the object of Caney's affections must have sensed her presence, for he raised his head, heretofore bent over his fiddle in concentration, and favored her with a brief, shy smile. That was enough for Caney; she was off to pursue the courtship.

Christy was startled back to attention when Mr. Vigil took her hand and placed it in the curve of his arm.

"You'll be wanting supper," he said. "The dining room is this way."

On the contrary, the *last* thing Christy wanted was food; she was far too worried about turning a corner and running into Zachary—when, precisely, had she begun to think of him as *Zachary* instead of *Mr. Shaw* or *the marshal*?—but she meant to make significant progress toward a successful marriage that evening, and if eating when she wasn't the least bit hungry was a part of it, she would endure.

"This is a splendid house," she said. "I must admit, I'm surprised to see such furnishings as these in a place as remote as Primrose Creek."

He frowned, but pleasantly, and led her toward a wide arched doorway. Beyond the threshold, people were gathered around a table that should have sagged, it held so many dishes. There were hams, a joint of beef, and mountains of fried chicken, along with all manner of sweets. "We're not so remote," he answered pleasantly. "San Francisco is only a few days from here in good weather, and there's talk that we'll be linked to the railroad soon."

The mention of San Francisco served to remind Christy of her mission, to send her sister to that great city, or one like it, for an education and a spectacular marriage. And that was a good thing, because she nearly collided with Zachary the moment she and Mr. Vigil stepped into the room.

He gave a slow whistle at the sight of her, Zachary did, and his eyes danced with mischief. Just then, someone drew Mr. Vigil away on some errand, and she was left with the man she least wanted to see.

"Go away," she whispered, snapping open her fan and waving it somewhat frantically back and forth under her chin.

He grinned, took in her gown, her carefully dressed hair, and the tasteful application of rouge on her mouth. "By all means," he said. "I wouldn't want to keep you from your work."

Chapter

4

I wouldn't want to keep you from your work.

Christy stared up at Zachary, aghast. Mr. Vigil's party spun at the edges of her vision, a dizzying whirl of color and sound and motion. Despite a deep personal aversion to violence of any kind, she was hard put not to slap the marshal across the face with enough force to set him back on the worn heels of his boots. "I beg your pardon?" she managed at last.

He looked mildly chagrined—and, unfortunately, breathtakingly handsome in his plain suit coat, cotton shirt, and trousers. He took her elbow in a light grasp, pulled her out of the center of the dining room and into a quieter corner. He thrust one hand through his hair, which somehow contrived to look perfect even though it was too long and mussed into the bargain.

"I'm sorry," he said. "It's just that—" He paused, and his jaw tightened momentarily while he struggled with some private emotion. "Christy, if you go through with what I think you're planning on doing, you'll be marrying a house, not a man, and ruining not only your life but Jake's, too."

"I must say," Christy sputtered, her fan still generating a furious breeze, "that you have your share of brass, and more, speaking to me this way. How *dare* you?"

He took her upper arms in his hands then, firmly, but not in a way that was uncomfortable. "You know damn well what I'm talking about," he rasped. "There's something between us, for right or for wrong, for better or for worse, and I for one want to know what it is while there's still time to do something about it!"

Christy averted her eyes, unable to meet his gaze, unable to pull out of his arms. When she looked at him again, it was through a blur of tears. "Only fools marry for passion," she said softly. Sadly. "For—for love." Hadn't she seen that for herself? Not once but twice?

"No," he countered in an outraged whisper. "Only fools marry for any *other* reason."

She thought of her home, with its dirt floor and chinked log walls. She might have been content once never to have anything more than that, if she had true love. Now, though, she knew how rare that was, and in point of fact, she would have preferred to remain unmarried, had she been given a choice. However, a lady without a husband was in a precarious position, not only socially but economically, too. The brothels and fancy houses were filled with women who, without property or private funds or a man to provide for them, protect them—be he brother, husband, or father—had nowhere else to turn.

"Christy," Zachary said, with a gentle squeeze on her upper arms. "Listen to me. I'm not asking you to stop seeing Jake. I'm not asking you to run off with me, though I've got to admit the idea has a measure of appeal, for me, at least. All I'm saying is that you shouldn't hurry into anything as important, as permanent—"

She straightened her spine, raised her chin, and stepped back. "You don't understand," she accused quietly, proudly. "You'll never understand, because you're a man, and you can get anything you want in this world if you're willing to try hard enough."

"Not anything," he corrected her. Then, with a look of defeat in his usually dancing, mischievous eyes, he offered her a broken smile, turned, and walked away, leaving her standing there in a corner of Jake Vigil's opulent dining room, staring after him. She felt exactly as she had when she'd first realized that the South she'd known, beloved home, refuge of her heart, had been trampled into the ground. She'd lost virtually everything and everyone that was important to her—Granddaddy, her mother, her father and uncle, and the farm—oh, dear heaven, *the farm,* the most beautiful place on earth, hidden away in an especially verdant corner of the Shenandoah Valley.

Now, oddly, Zachary Shaw seemed to be the greatest loss of all.

"Christy?"

She turned to see Bridget standing beside her, her blue eyes troubled.

"Is everything all right?" her cousin asked quietly when Christy didn't speak.

Christy bit down hard on her lower lip, then rummaged up a smile from the part of her soul where she kept a secret and ever-dwindling store of them. Oh, but she was so bloody sick of putting on a brave face, making the best of things, carrying on in the face of every trial. "Everything is perfect," she said.

Bridget looked skeptical, and a little annoyed, but she didn't press the matter. It was plain from her expression that she had better things to do than try to coax the truth out of someone who did not wish to give it. "The fried chicken is excellent," she said, lifting her china plate slightly to exhibit an array of sumptuous food. Then her gaze rose over Christy's shoulder, and a warm smile spread across her face. "Here's Jake now, with your supper," she said. "I'll just go and find Trace. Make sure he's not talking politics with somebody."

She and Mr. Vigil exchanged brief pleasantries, and then Bridget disappeared into the crowd. Christy was surprised to find herself feeling almost as stricken as she had when Zachary Shaw had walked away.

"It's a nice night out," Mr. Vigil said, reddening from the neck up in a slow flood of color. He was extraordinarily shy, Christy thought, with a certain fondness. "Maybe you'd like to take your supper in the porch swing?"

Christy drew a mental deep breath and smiled

with bright resolution. "That would be lovely," she said. She resisted an urge to look around for some sign of Zachary and took the plate from Jake's hand, fearing he was about to drop it on the Persian rug.

She was, in fact, aware of Zachary's gaze as she passed through the parlor with Jake. She could feel his regard through layers of fabric and flesh, muscle and bone. No force on earth could have made her seek him in that moment, and yet she was weak with the desire to do exactly that. Skye, too, was watching, her gaze fixed on Jake.

As Christy had noted on her first visit, the Vigil mansion was surrounded by a gracious veranda. On the moonward side, in the soft light from tall windows, the white bench swing swayed ever so slightly in the evening breeze. Although she was nervous, Christy knew she was perfectly safe in Jake's company, and she willingly took a seat at his bidding, her supper plate held carefully in her lap.

Jake joined her, his significant weight causing the wood and chain supports to complain a little. He did not meet her eyes but instead admired the spatter of bright silver stars winking in the sky. The clean scents of timber and freshly bathed and barbered man mingled pleasantly with those of party food and night air.

"It's been a long time since a pretty woman like you came through Primrose Creek," Jake said after a period of awkward silence. Even now, as he spoke, he didn't look at her but concentrated on the spectacular sky and the obviously painful task of courting. "A man gets lonesome. Begins to wonder why he's worked so hard, built himself a fine house—"

Christy waited, unable to speak and certainly unable to eat. She wanted to bolt to her feet and flee, but she remained. She had set her course, and she meant to follow it.

Jake cleared his throat. The poor man looked miserable, there in the lace-filtered light from the parlor windows behind them. "Things happen fast out here, ma'am," he said, and his voice was still gruff despite his efforts to the contrary. "What might take a year or two back east, well—what I'm trying to say is—"

Christy might not have loved Jake Vigil, but she certainly liked him. She was a good judge of character, normally, and all her instincts told her that this man was kind, honorable, and generous, as well as wealthy. He possessed all the qualities she sought in a husband—or, at least, most of them.

She took his hand, letting her plate rest untouched on her thighs, and encouraged him with a squeeze of her fingers.

"What I'm trying to say is, I'm the sort of man who needs a wife. I don't drink much, nor gamble, nor chase after women. I'd never beat you or force—force myself on you—" He nearly choked on this last, poor man. Christy's bruised and cautious heart warmed a little more. "I've got no debts to speak of, and plenty of money to provide for you and for our children. I'd like—" He swallowed, made another start. "I'd like your permission to court you proper, with an eye to our getting married soon as it's decent."

It was Christy's turn to swallow. This was what she'd wanted, what she'd aimed to achieve, but she had expected the matter to take longer and perhaps to be just a little more challenging. "You're welcome to come calling, Mr. Vigil."

He took her hand now and squeezed gently. "Jake," he said gruffly. "Please call me Jake."

She managed to look at him. "You know hardly anything at all about me," she said. "We're strangers."

He surprised her by raising her hand to his lips and brushing a light kiss across the backs of her knuckles. She felt nothing at all, though she knew that the same gesture from Zachary would have infused her with heat. "I'm an honest man," he said. "I'm thirty years old, and I've never been married. Never had the time. I thought when I built this house and ordered all those fancy things from San Francisco to fill it up, well, it would be like having a real home. What I learned was, it takes a wife to give a place life, and—in due time, of course—I'd like us to have a family."

Christy wanted a husband. She wanted a lovely home, too, and she *definitely* wanted children of her own. Jake, a fine man, had just declared his very respectable intentions, and yet she felt more sorrow than joy. Zachary's words in the dining room pulsed in her heart. *You'll be marrying a house, not a man, and ruining not only your own life but Jake's, too . . .*

She would *not* ruin Jake's life, she promised herself in that moment, nor her own. Her devotion, if not precisely genuine, would be unfailing and, in the spirit of Holy Scripture, her husband's heart would have cause to trust safely in her. "Yes," she said, practically forcing the word off her tongue. "Of course, we'll have children."

He smiled at her at long last, and she wished with all her soul that she might love him, that some benign force, dancing by on the scented breeze of a spring evening, would cause her truly to adore this shy, gentle man. "We're agreed, then?" he asked.

She nodded, looked away, then down at the plate of now-cold food resting forgotten on her lap. She had not eaten since breakfast, and yet she knew that one bite would send her dashing for the bushes.

The morning sunshine was like a spill of silvery fire on the waters of the creek, and Caney, crouched on the bank and busily scrubbing a pair of worn-out muslin bloomers, fairly pinned Christy to the trunk of a giant ponderosa pine, so intense was the look in her brown eyes. "That's just plain whorin'," she said, in her forthright way. "I'll have no part of it, Christy McQuarry. Mind you remember that. You go ahead with this lame-brained scheme of yours, and I'll move on without lookin' back. Leave you to simmer in your own brew. Don't you think I won't, neither."

Christy, equally busy with a set of much-mended linen sheets, was tired of defending her decision. "You wouldn't leave Primrose Creek," she said, a little peevishly. "You've set your heart on marrying up with Mr. Hicks, and it appears that he means to stay right where he is."

"I can be married to Mr. Malcolm Hicks and still

pick who I wants to socialize with, Miss Snippety-britches. And don't you go thinkin' you can sweet-talk me into keepin' house for you. I ain't about to do that. No, sir. I'll go on across the creek there and do for Trace and Miss Bridget and them babies, show you what's what."

Christy had secretly hoped to persuade Caney to come to work for her once she was Mrs. Jake Vigil, and she hadn't given up on the idea. Still, the idea of Caney abandoning her and Megan for Bridget brought stinging color to her cheeks and a flash of temper to her eyes. "Why don't you just go right on over there now," she replied, bluffing shamelessly, "if that's how you feel?"

A short, vibrant silence descended, and Caney relented first, if grudgingly. "Miss Megan needs me 'round here, since her own flesh and blood—you—don't have a lick of sense!"

Christy swished a soapy pillowcase in the water with perhaps more industry than was strictly necessary. After her marriage to Jake, she and Megan and Caney would live in a lovely, spacious house, where they belonged, where they were wanted and cared for and, most of all, safe. They would never want for anything again. Why couldn't Caney see that? Why couldn't Megan?

It galled Christy that Caney, whose opinion she valued above 'most every other, did not approve. "You're a free woman," she said tautly. "You may certainly do whatever you want."

Now, Caney looked more despondent than angry.

"You ain't gonna change your mind, neither, are you? I swear I've seen bulls with thinner skulls than you got."

Christy merely shook her head. No, she wasn't going to change her mind. She sought her younger sister out with her eyes, found her carrying buckets of water uphill to the lodge for cooking and washing up. Megan had already fed the mules and worked several hours in the garden, and although she did not seem unhappy, Christy could imagine only too well how years of such drudgery would steal the hope from Megan's heart, the spark from her green eyes, making her old and frail long before her time.

Christy could not bear the prospect, neither for her sister nor for herself, nor for the children she hoped to raise in a loving and unshakably secure home. The sort of life they'd all had before their world was torn apart.

"Let the girl find her own way," Caney said softly, evidently having followed Christy's thoughtful gaze. "The good Lord's got a plan for her, same as everybody else."

Christy's jaw clenched, unclenched. The Lord. She'd seen *His* plans before—for her granddaddy, for her mother, for the South, for the farm generations of McQuarrys had labored to build. She wasn't about to trust Him with something so vitally important as her younger sister's fate—or her own, for that matter. She held her tongue, however, for she knew the subject of God and His doings was of utmost importance to Caney; the other woman would rise up fierce as a fire-breathing dragon if roused to defend her beliefs.

It almost seemed that Caney read her mind in that moment; she stood, wrung out the bloomers she'd been washing, and turned to drape them over some bushes to dry. "I am goin' to town," she announced stiffly. "Don't wait supper on me."

Christy offered no protest; in truth, she was glad of the promise of some time alone with her thoughts. She finished the laundry and got to her feet, her knees and back sore from hard work, her skirts wet through, her hair tumbling from its pins.

Megan was crossing the footbridge, probably planning to pay Skye a visit, and Caney had saddled one of the mules and ridden off in a cloud of indignation and dust. Wearily, Christy began making her way up the hill toward the lodge. She planned to come back for the wash in a couple of hours; in the meantime, she would search the woods and fields for wild strawberries or perhaps a honeycomb.

The bees were out in force, and she spotted a large hive in the crotch of a tree, but catching a glimpse of a black bear, far off in the distance, Christy decided against the enterprise and continued her search for berries. She'd wandered some distance from the lodge when she came across a patch and stooped to begin picking the small, tart berries, using the front of her skirt for a basket. She smiled as she worked, remembering a similar venture back home in Virginia during her early childhood, when Granddaddy had accused her of eating more berries than she brought home, then laughed and lifted her high by the waist and spun her around and around until she was swoon-headed with delight.

It was the snuffle of a horse that made her realize she wasn't alone; she had not heard hoofbeats or the jingle of bridle fittings. She looked up and saw a fierce-looking Indian woman, white-haired and wrinkled, glaring down at her from the back of a sleek buckskin mare. Dressed in worn leather, the visitor carried a spear in one hand, and her eyes were black, bright as a crow's.

Christy was so taken aback that for several moments she didn't notice that the old woman was carrying something besides the spear. Her first thought was that she must be trespassing, and she was about to apologize, when the ancient rider leaned down from her horse and held out a squirming, whimpering bundle.

"Make well," she said, in a tone that brooked no argument. "White man's medicine, make well."

Christy was at once attracted and repelled. Curiosity drove her forward; she held out her arms, forgetting all about the berries she'd gathered, and found herself holding an infant wrapped in a horse blanket. The child was barely conscious; heat radiated from its copper-colored flesh, and the thick head of dark hair was matted with sweat.

"Wait," she said when the spell was broken and she raised her eyes from the baby's face. "I can't—I'm not—"

"You *make well,*" the old one reiterated, poking a gnarled and warning finger at Christy, knotty as the trunk of a time-twisted tree.

"But—"

The woman reined her horse around, spurred it with the heels of her moccasins, and was gone, her waist-length braid bobbing along the length of her rigid spine.

Christy pushed back the blanket and gazed down at a round, glistening little face. She'd helped Caney with various doctoring tasks on the road west with the wagon train, set some broken bones, and even removed the occasional bullet from the leg or shoulder of some hapless traveler. But for all that, she didn't have the remotest idea how to help this child.

After turning around in a full circle, she finally got her bearings and started toward home. She was three-quarters of the way there before it came to her that the baby might be—probably was—suffering from scarlet fever. That represented an acute danger to Megan, who had never had the dreaded malady, and of course to Bridget's young son, Noah, and even her unborn baby. Christy could not rightly remember whether she had had the disease or not. If she had, she'd been very small at the time.

She stopped. What should she do? She wouldn't have been able to abandon a well child, let alone a sick one. But neither did she wish to put so many other people at risk. If only Caney hadn't gone storming off to town, she would surely have had a practical suggestion to offer.

She began walking again, cutting through trees and brush toward the road that led to Primrose Creek. There was no real doctor in the immediate area, as far as she knew, but with luck she might encounter Caney returning from her highly improper visit to Mr. Malcolm Hicks.

Instead, she ran into Trace, driving a buckboard loaded with building supplies. Seeing Christy, he grinned and drew back on the reins, bringing the team of mismatched horses to a stop. He set the brake lever with a motion of one foot. "Hullo," he said. His expression turned solemn when he realized she was carrying something in her arms, and he started to jump down in order to approach her. "There'll be a fellow out to collect those army horses," he said. "Name's Charlie Brimm. He's headed down Fort Grant way and said he'd be glad to take them back."

The two horses she and Megan had borrowed were the last thing she cared about just then. "Stop, Trace," she said clearly and very firmly. "Don't come any closer."

He frowned, pushed his hat to the back of his head. "What—?"

She folded back the saddle blanket, at least far enough to reveal the baby. "He—or she—is very ill. I think it might be scarlet fever."

Trace let out a long, low whistle. "Good Lord," he breathed. "Where did you get him?"

Christy explained hastily. "Is there a doctor *anywhere* nearby?" she asked desperately, just in case.

Trace shook his head. "Closest one is Doc Tatum, down at Fort Grant. And he's not going to come near a baby with scarlet fever, in case of an epidemic on his own ground. You might try the Arrons, though—up at the mission. The reverend used to practice medicine before he took up preaching to the heathens."

"Doctor Tatum would turn an ailing child away? I'll bet he'd tend a *white* child," Christy said shortly. She knew she was being unfair, but frustration and fear had never had a worthy effect on her character.

"That may be so," Trace allowed, and he looked as stricken by the knowledge as Christy felt. "Best try the Arrons, though. I hear they did a lot of good a couple of years back when the diphtheria struck. Fact is, they'd probably take the little fellow in for good."

Would they? Christy wondered. Or would she and the child travel all that way, through unfamiliar and dangerous territory, only to be turned away? She had made the acquaintance of any number of dedicated missionaries in her travels up to then, but she had also run across a few who'd made her wonder if hellfire, or at least purgatory, wouldn't be preferable to an eternity spent in their company.

"You can't go alone," Trace said when she didn't speak. "I'll let Bridget know we'll be gone a day or two and ride over there with you myself."

Christy was shaking her head before he'd finished making the statement. "And take a chance on infecting Noah or the new baby? Absolutely not."

"Then what?"

"Caney and I will go. She's bound to be back from town soon."

"I wouldn't count on that," Trace replied with just the slightest hint of a grin touching one corner of his mouth. "I just saw her, heading out of town in a buggy with Malcolm. I believe they might be planning to have a picnic supper together somewhere private. Play hell finding them."

Only dogged determination kept Christy standing; she wanted to sit down by the wayside, the sick baby still in her arms, and wail disconsolately. As usual, though, she did not have that luxury. "I've got to do *something,*" she said, as much to herself as to Trace. "I can't just give up and let this child die—"

Trace was bringing the buckboard around in a broad, noisy circle. "I'll head back and try to find Caney. Megan can stay at our place until you get back."

"Thank you," Christy said with a long sigh. As Trace and his team and wagon disappeared into a dusty cloud, she found a seat on a fallen log and rocked the baby back and forth, back and forth, singing a wordless lullaby.

Considerable time had passed, though Christy never knew how much, before Trace returned, not with Caney but with Marshal Zachary Shaw. The lawman rode that magnificent brown-and-tan stallion of his and led a dappled gray mare, no doubt borrowed, behind him.

"Where," Christy demanded, standing up and then sitting down again, "is Caney?"

"She's a mite busy," the marshal said, with a smile that was civil and no more. "Man cut his arm half off in Jake's mill about half an hour back. Caney's stitching up the gash." He swung down from the saddle and came toward her, apparently unconcerned about the possibilities of contagion. "Anyhow, the way to the mission isn't safe for a couple of women traveling alone."

Trace took off his hat, wiped his forehead with one arm, and watched the interchange carefully, like somebody staring up at the night sky on Independence Day, anticipating fireworks. "Bridget and I will see to Megan and Caney," he said. "You two had better get started while you've still got a few hours of daylight left."

Had Christy not been wretched with worry over the child, she would have marveled at her ill fortune. First, she'd had to endure Zachary Shaw's company during the long ride up the mountain from Fort Grant. Now, the two of them would be on the trail together again, for who knew how long, or under what circumstances, with only a very sick infant for a chaperone. It seemed to her that she had quite enough problems, thank you very much, without having to deal with this particular man on top of everything else.

"Let's see," he said, and, to her surprise, reached out and took the baby from her arms as easily as if he'd already raised a houseful of them. He turned back a corner of the saddle blanket and spoke quietly. "Hullo there, buckaroo. I hear tell you've come for a visit. Feeling a little rough, are you?"

Christy's throat tightened with an emotion she couldn't define. "I guess we'd better get started," she said with resignation. Heaven only knew what this undertaking was going to do to her marriage plans. Jake was unlikely to approve of such a journey, no matter how noble her reasons for making it. It wasn't as if she had a viable choice, though, given the circumstances.

"I suppose he ought to have water," she said weakly.

Trace called out a farewell just then and rattled away toward home.

"I've got a canteen on my saddle," Zachary replied. "I'll hold him while you mount up, then I'll hand him over."

She gathered the gray's reins in one hand and climbed easily onto the animal's back. Zachary gave her the baby when she was settled in the saddle and then soaked what she hoped was a clean handkerchief in water from his canteen and passed that to her, too.

Christy put the end of the handkerchief gently into the child's mouth, and he whimpered fitfully and began to suckle weakly. Zachary gave her the canteen when she was ready to accept it and then reined his stallion toward the higher peaks to the west.

"We might reach the mission around midnight," he said, "if you can keep up."

Christy would not allow him to nettle her. She spurred the mare into a trot alongside Zachary. "Where did you learn to do that?" she asked.

"Do what?" he replied. His eyes were so blue it hurt to look into them, the way it sometimes hurt to look up at a vivid sky.

She kept the baby in a tight, careful grasp, controlling the reins with one hand. "You're at ease around babies. Why is that?"

He grinned, adjusted his hat. "I grew up in a big family. Five younger, five older. We all helped out."

She was grateful that the conversation had taken a relatively harmless turn. "Where? I mean, where did you live?"

"We started out in Sioux City, then moved on to Denver when I was fourteen," he answered. "Took two wagons just to haul us all. My father was a preacher, an undertaker, a blacksmith, and a sometime-dentist, too, when the situation called for it. We never had much, but we didn't do without anything, either."

"Your mother?"

"She's still in Denver. Lives with my eldest brother and his wife. The rest of us are scattered from one end of creation to the other."

Christy was struck by the easy affection in his voice and expression. Whatever the privations involved, the Shaw family had obviously been a happy one. She envied him that. "What made you leave Denver?"

They had reached a flat stretch of trail, and their horses moved naturally into a gallop. Zachary's eyes turned thoughtful, maybe even a little evasive, but in the end he answered. "A woman," he said.

Christy wished she hadn't asked. Had she truly imagined, for so much as a moment, that such a man might have reached adulthood without courting someone? Still, the thought of Zachary Shaw romancing anyone else was nearly intolerable, even though she most certainly didn't want him for herself. "Ah," she replied at some length. "I'm sorry. I didn't mean to pry."

"I don't mind telling you," he answered easily. "Her name was Jessie St. Clair. She and I were planning on being married. She went into the bank one day, to deposit the day's profits from her father's mercantile, and walked straight into the middle of a robbery." He paused. Looked away. "She was shot. Killed instantly."

Christy felt ill, not to mention guilty for resenting a dead woman, taken long before her time. "I'm so sorry," she said.

"Wasn't your fault," he replied flatly. "You going to be able to hold on to that baby? Or should I rig up some kind of sling?"

"I can hold him for a while," she answered. "Did you love her?" Now, what—*what*—had made her ask such a personal question?

He looked into her eyes, intensely and for a long time. "Yes," he said. "I loved her. Now, tell me exactly how you came by this baby. Trace's story was a little short on detail."

Christy explained how she'd been picking berries and encountered the old woman. "They'll kill me if this child dies, won't they?" she said. The realization, having nagged at her all along, finally struck home. "The Indians, I mean."

Zachary didn't smile, but he didn't look worried, either. "I reckon they'll try," he said.

They traveled mostly in silence after that and stopped beside a mountain spring several hours later to water the horses. While they were resting, he asked for her petticoat and quickly made a sturdy sling in which to carry the baby safely and without undue strain on Christy's arms and back. They had, by that time, discovered that the "little fellow" was a girl.

"I've been wondering about something," Zachary said when they were ready to move on. He had donned the sling himself, the baby couched comfortably inside, and mounted the stallion.

Christy sighed. "What?" She was tired, sore, and terribly afraid for the infant girl fate had put in her charge. She lifted herself into the saddle and took up the reins.

"Where did you learn to ride the way you do? You sit a horse like an Indian."

She smiled. Her eyes were hot with exhaustion, her heart ached, she was hungry, and it would be hours before they reached their destination. "I was raised on a farm in Virginia," she told him. "I can't remember a time when I wasn't around horses—in fact, I was probably riding before I could walk. My daddy would have seen to that."

"Tell me about him."

It was only fair. He'd volunteered considerable information about his own family, and she had no good reason not to speak of hers. "My daddy's name was Eli McQuarry. He was a rascal from the day he was born. He drank enough for himself and half the county and rode like the devil was after him most of the time. He and Uncle J.R. got into a duel over a woman, and right after that, Mama lit out for England with a man she met in Richmond. A baron. She dragged Megan and me right along with her."

She'd revealed far more than she'd intended, but there was no help for it.

"Did you like living over there?"

She shook her head. "I was so homesick for Virginia, and for my granddaddy, that sometimes I thought I'd die of it."

His face and hair seemed gilded by the afternoon sunshine, and his profile glowed. He supported the baby girl, in her petticoat pouch, with one arm. "Are you still? Homesick, I mean?"

Christy examined her heart and took her time about it.

"No," she said finally. "It's not the same anymore."

He shook his head in acknowledgment and turned to look at her, but she couldn't see his expression because most of his face was cast in shadow by the brim of his hat. "So Primrose Creek is home now?"

She didn't avert her eyes, though the temptation was strong. "Yes," she said. "Primrose Creek is home."

Chapter 5

Christy's first glimpse of the lake, a sapphire in a setting of trees, mountains, and sky, quite literally took her breath away. She could not speak for a long time but simply stood in her stirrups, taking in the astounding vista before her. A sense of deep reverence came over her, and she wanted to weep, not from sorrow but from joy.

As the sun set the horizon ablaze, splashes of silver and crimson, gold and purple danced over the otherwise placid surface of the water.

Zachary, still carrying the baby, reined in beside her. "The locals call it Tahoe," he said. "That's a twist on a Washoe word whites can't pronounce. To a lot of Indians, it's simply 'Lake of the Sky.' "

Christy let out a long, tremulous breath. Indeed, the latter was a fitting description, for one might have thought the sky itself had come fluttering down to earth in silken billows of blue, to settle gracefully into the midst of grandeur. "I have never seen anything so beautiful," she managed. "Never."

She felt his smile before she caught sight of it out of the corner of her eye. "Makes a person think there must be a God," he said. "There's no other way to explain something like this."

"I never want to leave," Christy whispered, still spellbound. "I wish I could build a cabin right here and spend the rest of my life just looking."

Zachary chuckled, a low and masculine sound, probably common and yet seeming to belong only to him. Against his midsection, the baby began to whimper, like some small, desolate, wounded creature of the woods, driven out of its hiding place and into open and very dangerous territory.

"Shhh, now," he said to the baby, and, miraculously, the child quieted. His expression was serious when he turned to look at Christy. "Maybe you can have your wish, after a fashion," he said, with all the eagerness of someone about to be thrown from his horse in the middle of a cattle stampede. "This little bit of a lady needs to stop and rest. So do you, for that matter."

Christy couldn't refute his statement. They had been riding for hours, and the baby was surely not only gravely ill but exhausted as well. She, too, was tired, although she'd worked and driven the wagon many times in much worse condition. "I'll give the child more water," she said, "while you see to the horses and build a fire."

He grinned. "Yes, your ladyship," he said, and tugged at his hat brim.

She frowned, unamused. "Why do you always

have to do that? Mock me as though I were some supercilious dowager ordering you about, I mean?"

The grin stuck and rose to dance in his eyes. "I like to watch your reaction," he answered, swinging easily down from the saddle to stand looking up at her. "Besides, you *do* have a tendency to give unnecessary instructions and unsolicited advice."

Christy made a point of refusing his help when she dismounted, not because she was angry—she wasn't particularly—but because she desperately needed to maintain some illusion of distance between them. When she was standing on the ground, facing Zachary, he carefully removed the sling from around his neck and handed her the baby.

"I'll make camp," he said.

Christy merely nodded, turned on one heel, and walked away. There was a small clearing a few yards away, full of deep, luscious grass and spring wildflowers. She found a bit of soft ground and knelt, laying the child down before her and tenderly unwrapping her from the ruined petticoat and the horse blanket beneath.

There were sores from one end of the tiny body to the other, and the little girl's flesh was so hot that Christy could have warmed her hands from several inches away. A sound of despair escaped her, and the baby opened luminous brown eyes to gaze up into her face. The little one's expression was wretched; though not more than eight or nine months old, this child knew she was likely to die and wanted very much to live.

Tears burning her eyes, Christy tore off a small piece of the petticoat sling, moistened it with canteen water, and carefully bathed the baby's sore-covered skin, hoping to ease the fever a little and somehow communicate her own determination to fight the disease to the end.

"She ought to have a name," Zachary said from behind her. "Don't you think?"

Christy had finished bathing the infant, fashioned a diaper of sorts from another piece of the petticoat, and wrapped the baby in the horse blanket. She had been kneeling there, facing the lake like a supplicant praying to a saint, holding the child in her arms, and she'd had no sense of the passage of time. Now, though, she heard the crackle of a small fire and smelled wood smoke. "Yes," she said. "A name."

Zachary helped her to her feet. "Any suggestions?"

Christy could not think beyond the strange turmoil inside her, a tempest made of hope that the baby would recover, fear of the repercussions if she didn't, regret of various kinds, and a very real attraction to Zachary Shaw that seemed a holy thing, like the lake itself. "Jenny," she said. "My—my mother was called Jenny."

He smoothed a tendril of hair at her temple, his touch light as the passing breeze. "Jenny it is, then," he agreed. " 'Course, we've got to remember that she belongs to somebody. No question about it, they'll be back to claim her once she's hale and hearty again."

It was bittersweet, the experience of caring for a child, naming her, with Zachary's help. Christy loved children of all ages, always had. At the same time, it hurt far more than she would ever have guessed, knowing this was all she would ever have of motherhood—with this man at her side, anyway. "Yes," she answered at long last, and felt the word catch in her throat.

He caressed her cheek. "Everything's going to be all right," he said quietly, and it seemed to Christy that he was talking about more than little Jenny's recovery. Then he walked away, pulled his rifle from its scabbard, laid his .45 on a fallen log near the fire. "I'll find us some supper," he said. "If you get any visitors in the meantime, make sure that pistol is within easy reach."

Christy looked askance at the gun. "I've never—"

"And you probably won't have to fire it. But if anything or anybody comes around bothering you, pick the thing up, point it at them, and, if you have to, pull the trigger."

She shivered. "All—all right. But hurry."

That wicked grin came again. "Are you going to miss me?"

"No," she lied. "I'm hungry, that's all."

Zachary laughed and disappeared into the timber on foot. The stallion and the mare were hobbled nearby, where they could graze in the sweet grass and drink from the lake.

Christy paced awhile, Jenny fitful in her arms, then sat down on the same log where the pistol rested, keeping a careful distance. She gave the baby as much water as she would take, rocked her, and sang soft snippets of lullabies she remembered from her own childhood.

Presently, she heard a shot in the near distance and moved a little closer to the pistol, in case the report had not been that of Zachary's rifle sighted in on their supper. Twenty minutes later, he reappeared, carrying the gun in one hand and two skinned rabbits in the other.

While he rigged up a spit over the fire and put the meat on to roast, Christy did her level best to think only of Jake Vigil. The trouble was, she couldn't call his image to mind, let alone the touch of his hand or the sound of his voice. She was full of Zachary, as full of him as the lake was of sky, and fearful that she would never exorcise him from her mind and spirit.

He watched Christy through his lashes while he whittled idly at a stick, beside the fire, thinking she looked like an angel, sitting there on that log, holding little Jenny with an air of weary defiance, as if to inform the universe that she would not surrender her charge, even to death. She'd eaten hardly anything, despite an earlier claim that she was hungry, and she looked like a waif in her rumpled dress with her glossy dark hair falling around her straight little shoulders.

He felt something powerful, and if it wasn't love, it was something damn close. It stirred an odd mingling of joy and despair within him, that mysterious sentiment, and scared the hell out of him, but he faced it squarely all the same. When he'd knelt beside Jessie in that Denver bank, holding her lifeless body in his arms, refusing to let go until his father and two of his older brothers came to pry him away, he'd sworn there would never be another woman for him.

There had been a few passing fancies, of course. Whores, good-hearted and otherwise, the occasional widow, even an unhappy wife or two. He'd always been able to tip his hat and ride away when it was over, without a second thought or a backward look. This time, he was going to get his heart broken, for sure and for certain, and probably for life. Watching Christy marry Jake Vigil would be almost as bad as feeling Jessie's life seep, crimson, into the front of his shirt and the legs of his trousers.

He'd given a lot of thought to the matter of Christy McQuarry, especially after seeing her step out onto the veranda with Jake the night before during that blasted party of his. It had been all he could do not to storm out there and fling Vigil over the porch railing, just as if he had the right. Just as if Jake wasn't one of his closest friends.

He sighed. It was going to happen, and he might as well accept the fact. Christy meant to hitch up with Jake, even though she didn't love him, because of the money and the house and the prestige of being married to a man of substance. It might have been easier if he thought her motivation was greed, and he had to admit the thought had crossed his mind. He could have despised her then—but he knew better. Christy had seen her world fold up and cave in on itself and gotten a taste of true devastation, and somewhere along the line she'd gotten the crazy idea that she could avoid further losses by cushioning herself with money.

He continued to whittle. Back in Primrose Creek, on his desk at the jailhouse, was a stack of wanted posters. He'd been studying them thoughtfully when Trace came to fetch him; some of the rewards amounted to a small fortune. If he talked fast enough, he might be able to chide the mayor and the town council into hiring a temporary deputy to make his rounds while he did a little bounty hunting. . . .

"Do you think she'll die?"

He looked up, caught off guard by the question. It was a moment before he realized she was talking about the child they'd dubbed Jenny. He cleared his throat before answering. "I reckon we need to be prepared for the possibility," he said. "But she's obviously a tough little character. A lot of babies wouldn't have made it this far."

"I keep thinking it was a mistake, taking her on a difficult journey like this," Christy fretted.

"What else could you have done?"

He watched her as she studied the child. Her heart was visible in her face, in the tremulous motion of her hand as she soothed the small brow. He ached with the need to spare her the sorrow she was courting and knew, at the same time, that it could not be done.

She didn't look up. "I don't know. There was no place in town where I could take her, and if I'd brought her back to the lodge, Megan might have become infected."

"What about you?"

At last, she met his eyes, looking puzzled and worn-out enough to drop. "I don't understand."

"Are you immune to scarlet fever, Christy?" The answer was more important to him than his next heartbeat. He wondered why he hadn't asked before and concluded that he'd been afraid of the answer.

He knew by her hesitation, by the way she ran the tip of her tongue nervously over her lips, by the wobbling smile that made a brief landing on her mouth before taking wing and disappearing, but he still held his breath until she spoke.

"I don't recall ever having it. There was an outbreak of diphtheria when we were traveling with the wagon train, and once, cholera. I helped Caney with the sick but never fell ill myself." She swallowed visibly. "And you, Zachary? Have you had it?"

He nodded. "Yep. We had an epidemic in Denver when I was a kid. Nobody died, not in our family, at least, but two of my sisters are hard of hearing, and my youngest brother was left with a weak heart." He gave her a few moments to collect herself, for she was plainly on the verge of panic. He set his whittling aside. "Here," he said quietly. "Let me look after Miss Jenny for a while. You need to rest."

She hesitated, then surrendered the child and went down to the lake to splash her face and hands and stare out at the view.

Zachary put down a desire to follow and take Christy in his arms and hold her, but just barely. He got his canteen and ferreted a bent spoon out of the depths of his saddle bags, all the while holding the baby in one arm.

He was sitting under a tree, knees bent, with Jenny resting on his thighs while he fed her droplets of water from the spoon. He didn't hear Christy come back, he was so intent on the task.

"You're a good man, Zachary," she said, as though there had ever been any doubt.

He grinned ruefully. "Yeah. That and a nickel will get me a shot of whiskey at the Golden Garter." He gave Jenny more water. "I've only got one blanket," he said, braced for the inevitable protest. "We're going to have to share it, I guess."

Once again, she surprised him. "After this, my reputation will probably be in shreds anyway," she said. "But don't mistake me, Marshal. I still plan to marry Jake Vigil if he'll have me, and I'll countenance no nonsense from you."

He might have laughed, if it hadn't been for the fact that he wanted her so badly. "Jake is no fool," he said. "He'd have you if you grew another head. 'Course, he might shoot me just for being here, but I don't imagine you'd let a little thing like that spoil your wedding day."

She made everything infinitely worse by smiling down at him. "Thank you," she said. "Thank you for caring enough to escort Jenny and me to the mission. I know a lot of people wouldn't have."

Her gratitude undid him in a whole new way. Evidently, she was just brimming with ways to turn him inside out. "Some folks don't have much use for

Indians," he allowed, looking at the child and feeling a profound mixture of fury and sorrow at the injustice of it all.

It was probably a good thing Christy was bound to marry Jake instead of him. Maybe in five years—maybe in a hundred—he'd be glad he'd been spared a lifetime of Christy McQuarry.

Zachary had made a bed for the three of them on a cushion of soft grass, using their saddle blankets as an improvised mattress. Christy and the baby were snuggled beneath his bedroll when he sat down on the ground to pull off his boots. Overhead, a sky full of stars gleamed and winked, like diamonds scattered across a length of midnight-blue velvet, and the light of a full-to-bursting moon shimmered upon the waters of the lake.

She did not expect to sleep, but gradually her exhaustion pulled her under, and she surrendered to it. The baby's cry awakened her to a crisp, dew-laden morning. Zachary had already left the bed, and she could hear a new fire crackling, smell smoke and something delicious cooking.

Jenny was still weak, still in grave danger. But she was alive, and that was cause for celebration. Surely it was a good sign, her surviving this long. After improvising another diaper to replace the wet one, then tucking the baby into bed again until the sun was higher and the air warmer, Christy washed her own face and hands at the lakeside. Zachary was standing near the fire, watching her.

"Sorry I can't offer you hot coffee," he said. He was holding a long stick over the fire, with a fish crisping on its pointed end. "But there's trout for breakfast."

They ate with their fingers, watching sunlight spill further and further over the lake, then Zachary smothered the fire with dirt and saddled the horses while Christy put on the sling and placed Jenny inside it. She could feel the heat of the baby's fever, surely higher than before, even through her clothes, and fresh fear loomed up inside her, sudden and fierce. She faced the terror, as she had done many times before in her life, stared it down, but the task wasn't an easy one, and it left her a little dizzy.

Soon, they were mounted again and riding around the northern rim of the lake at a good pace. The beauty of their surroundings gave Christy a certain solace, and by the time the mission came into view, she was feeling strong again.

The mission building was a simple log structure, with a crude wooden cross standing prominently on its roof, and while there was no sign of activity outside, smoke curled from one of its two chimneys, and the front door stood open to the crisp, clean morning air.

Christy glanced at Zachary, expecting to see her own relief reflected in his face. Instead, he looked solemn.

"Is something wrong?" she asked, frowning a little. Jenny fidgeted against her middle and gave a mewling cry.

Zachary removed his hat and replaced it in an agitated fashion. "I hope not," he said, but his eyes were narrowed as he regarded the mission, and there was a certain intensity in his bearing that made her very nervous. He pulled his rifle from the scabbard at the side of his saddle and cocked it before drawing the .45 and handing it to Christy.

"Stay behind me," he said.

Christy's throat tightened painfully, and her palm was already sweating around the handle of that dreadful pistol, but she nodded. "All right," she croaked, holding Jenny a little closer.

They rode single file down the trail leading to the mission. Christy was expecting disaster at every moment; she could barely breathe, and her heart was pounding, but she held on to the .45 and the baby and kept her horse close behind Zachary's.

In the dusty dooryard, Zachary raised one hand to Christy in a silent command to stay put and be quiet, and he dismounted with the merest squeak of leather. Slowly, watchfully, he approached the open door. By that time, Christy shared his concern; visitors were surely rare in this isolated if beautiful place, and it seemed to her that someone should have come out to greet them by now.

He glanced back at Christy once, then stepped over the high threshold. A full two minutes passed before he came outside again, and Christy knew by the look on his face that he didn't have good news.

Unconsciously, she stood in her stirrups and leaned forward, as if by doing so she'd be able to see inside the mission. Find something that would prove him wrong.

"Probably Paiutes," he said, breaking the awful silence. "This is their territory. Reverend and Mrs. Arron are both dead."

Christy grasped the saddle horn with both hands and drew a slow, deep breath in an effort to steady herself. "Dear God," she whispered. "Are—are you sure?"

"Oh, yes," Zachary replied, leaning against the jamb of the door for a moment. "The reverend's got an arrow through his throat, and Mrs. Arron had her head beaten in with a rock."

Christy squeezed her eyes shut, fought back a rush of bile from her stomach. "What do we do now?" she whispered.

"Bury them," he said simply.

Belatedly, Christy realized that the Arrons' attackers might still be nearby, and she hastily looked back over one shoulder. The towering ponderosa pines, so magnificent before, now seemed sinister, as though they were concealing new violence.

"Stay outside," Zachary instructed. "Things are pretty ugly in here. I'll see to the bodies."

Christy was already climbing down from the saddle, one arm clenched tightly around the baby as she did so. "I've seen dead people before," she said staunchly. "I'll help."

He opened his mouth to warn her off again, then shook his head and retreated back into the mission. Christy followed and was nearly overwhelmed by the smell of death. The place was awash in blood, and the bodies were just as Zachary had described them, and so much worse.

Christy hastened outside, still carrying Jenny in the sling, and was violently ill, but she made herself go back into the cabin as soon as she'd regained her composure. Indian attacks were a grim reality of life on the frontier; she had seen atrocities before, when the wagon train had overtaken such horrors along the trail, but it wasn't the sort of discovery a person ever got used to. Faced with this carnage, she couldn't help imagining what vengeance the old Indian woman might bring down on her and Caney and, dear God, Megan, should she fail to save this baby.

When she rejoined Zachary, he had removed the arrow from the reverend's throat and wrapped both bodies in blankets. Without a word, Christy laid the baby on the Arrons' bed, placed pillows on either side for safety's sake, and then put water on the stove to heat. When it was hot, she found some rags and set herself to the task of cleaning up the evidence of murder.

Zachary was gone a long time, and when he returned, shovel in hand, his sleeves were rolled up and his clothes were dirty. He'd left his coat somewhere, and he looked haggard. Pale. He glanced around the cabin with weary appreciation.

"Thanks," he said. "I'm not sure I could have stomached any more just now."

Christy nodded, went to the stove, and poured him a cup of the coffee she'd made after setting the cabin to rights. Something had been puzzling her since their arrival inside the cabin. Mrs. Arron had shed lots of blood, but there had been hardly any in the place where the reverend lay.

"I'd say the reverend was shot someplace else," he said, as if reading her thoughts. "Whoever did it probably brought the body home before killing Mrs. Arron."

"So horrible," Christy murmured.

"How's the baby?"

"She still has a fever," Christy answered. "I was just about to bathe her with cool water again."

"I'll find the reverend's doctoring bag," Zachary said between sips of coffee. "Must be some medicine around here someplace." He paused, nodded toward a window. "There's a cow grazing out there. I'll get some milk, and we'll try feeding Jenny with a spoon."

The image of him sitting under a tree spooning water into the child's mouth rose before her mind's eye. She bit down hard on her lower lip and nodded, then fled into the cabin's tiny lean-to bedroom to attend to Jenny. The child's small body was limp with fever, and when Christy lifted her into her arms, the dark eyes rolled back until she could see only the whites.

Zachary brought in the reverend's medical bag, and there was a small vial of quinine inside, but Caney had told her repeatedly never to give an unconscious person water or medicine. Terrified, she frantically peeled off the shirtwaist she'd borrowed from Mrs. Arron's modest wardrobe to serve as a nightgown for the baby, grasped the basin from the wash table, and began once again to swab the infant's hot, ravaged flesh with cool water. This seemed to revive Jenny some, and Christy took the opportunity to give the weary baby as much of the quinine as she could tolerate. All the while, she prayed silently for a miracle, prayed even though she didn't think anyone was listening, even though her granddaddy had died and the farm was gone, even though the South had fallen, even though she was going to marry a man she didn't love.

Christy had curled up on the Arrons' bed and fallen into a sound sleep, and the child was snuggled against her middle, kicking and waving small, plump arms. Her eyes were bright, and she managed a faltering baby smile as she looked up at Zachary.

He had to deal with a whole tangle of feelings before he dared speak. "So you're feeling better, are you?" he asked quietly. When he extended a hand toward the baby and she clasped his finger, a sheen of tears blurred his vision. Nightfall was hours away, and already it had been one hell of a day.

Christy stirred, stretched, awakening slowly.

Zachary's insides ground with the desire to undress this complicated, irritating woman, make love to her, start a baby of their own. The first of many.

She sat up, looking rumpled and alarmed and entirely delectable. "Wh-what time is it?"

"On toward four in the afternoon," he answered. "Looks like your partner here is on the mend."

The look on her face when she realized that Jenny's fever had broken was as magnificent as a sunrise. She touched the baby's face and beamed up at him. "She is! She *is* better!"

He bent, kissed the top of Christy's head. He'd probably regret it, sooner or later—most likely sooner—but for the moment, it didn't seem like too much to ask, even in a hopeless situation like theirs.

"I caught the cow," he said, and immediately felt like an idiot.

She smiled at his expression. "Good. Jenny needs milk, so she can get her strength back. Don't you, little one?"

Minutes later, in the main part of the cabin, he watched, stricken, as Christy sat in Mrs. Arron's rocking chair, patiently spooning milk onto the baby's tongue, a few drops at a time. When Jenny drifted off into a healthy, natural sleep, she gazed serenely down at the child's peaceful little face and continued to rock gently back and forth.

Zachary's throat hurt, and for one moment, he wondered if he was coming down with scarlet fever for the second time in his life. Then, with an inward smile, he told himself he was coming down with something, all right, and no amount of quinine was going to cure it.

Christy carried the baby into the bedroom when she fell asleep in her arms, then returned momentarily to stand looking out the window. "Do you think they're out there?"

She was referring to the Arrons' killers, of course. He sighed, poured himself more coffee. Left over from earlier in the day, it was already stale, but it packed enough of a wallop to keep him on his feet. "Oh, yeah," he said grimly. "They're out there, all right."

"You're sure they were Indians?"

"Renegades, probably. But Indians, yes. The arrow was Paiute."

"We're in danger, then."

There was no sense in dodging the truth. "Yes."

"They could have attacked us while we were on the trail. Or camped last night by the lake."

"Yes," he repeated. "But they didn't. Apparently, they were busy elsewhere."

Her eyes filled with tears, and she looked away, blinking rapidly. "It must have been horrible—"

There was nothing to say to that. The Arrons had suffered, though probably briefly, and the brutality of such an attack was hard to get past. He'd seen worse, of course, but some things a man kept to himself.

"They might kill us that way," she said.

"I'll look after you," he replied.

"The reverend probably made the same promise to his wife."

"Christy, we can't stay here the rest of our lives. We've got to go back to Primrose Creek *sometime,* even if it means facing down a band of Paiutes."

She shivered at the prospect, and she was a little pale, but her head was high and her shoulders were straight. She sat down in the rocking chair again, her legs curled beneath her. "You're right. But I'm scared."

"So am I, if it's any comfort," he said.

She gave another shaky smile. "It isn't," she replied. "When are we leaving?"

He thought. "Tomorrow morning, I guess. If the baby is well enough, that is."

She nodded. "In the meantime—"

"In the meantime, we stay here. You and Jenny can have the bed, and I'll sleep in a chair."

She looked away, started to say something, stopped herself. Met his gaze again. "What about the horses? Are they safe?"

"About as safe as can be expected. I fed and watered them and put them up in the barn with the Arrons' cow. The reverend had a couple of mares and a gelding, last I knew, but they're gone. No surprise there."

She swallowed in an obvious effort to control a surge of well-justified fright. "It doesn't seem right, for their killers to go unpunished."

"Once we get back, I'll report the Arrons' murders to the army. They'll send out a few patrols, but like as not, nothing will come of it. And if it does—" He paused. "A couple of years back, down near Denver, some Indians killed a family of settlers. The law-abiding white folks took up arms and went out to avenge their friends and neighbors. They wiped out a village full of innocent women and children. In time, the braves gathered a war party and retaliated—it seems they'd been off someplace hunting when the first raids were made. If the army hadn't interceded, God knows where it would have ended."

"I've read some dreadful things." She nodded, glanced uneasily toward the windows. "Things Indians will do, I mean."

He approached her, laid a hand on her shoulder. "I'll take you home tomorrow, Christy," he said gruffly. "And you'll get there in one piece. You have my word on that."

She touched his fingers with her own, lightly, and fire shot through him.

"I believe you," she said.

Christy made a supper of sorts from potatoes and onions found in the Arrons' root cellar, and she brewed fresh coffee. She'd fashioned diapers from a muslin bed sheet—tragically, it would never be missed—and given Jenny more milk and, once it had cooled, some of the water she'd used to boil the potatoes.

While she and Zachary ate, alone at the well-worn table where countless graces had surely been offered, Christy listened to the howls of distant coyotes and wondered, were they really coyotes, or Indians calling to each other?

"Christy," Zachary said.

He'd been reading her face. She looked at him, tried to smile. "What?"

"Don't let your imagination run away with you. Indians usually don't attack at night. Something about spirits and ancestors."

"Then why aren't we traveling now? Why wait for daylight?"

Zachary heaved a sigh, and she realized how spent he must be after discovering the bodies and burying both Reverend and Mrs. Arron without help. "We can't risk taking that baby over the trail so soon. It's a miracle she made it as it stands."

She considered that. Considered the two devout people who had spent their lives in service to others and died at the hands of savages for their trouble. Two lives taken, one spared. The unbelievable beauty of the landscape, the ugliness of a cabin splashed with blood. Sometimes it was hard to know whether to despair or be thankful—creation seemed to be one big paradox.

Indeed, the ways of the Lord were past finding out.

Chapter 6

Through most of the night, Christy lay in the Arrons' bed, staring up at the dark ceiling and following every sound she heard through a labyrinth of possible horrors. Occasionally, she heard a creak from Zachary's rocking chair, and each time she took fresh comfort in his presence. Although she was most definitely afraid, she felt safer with him than she would have with a whole platoon from Fort Grant.

When morning came, and it took its sweet time, Christy was numb with exhaustion, and she counted that as a blessing. The day ahead was sure to be a difficult one, and the effects of a sleepless night might serve as a sort of buffer to her already raw emotions.

Zachary turned the Arrons' cow loose before they rode out, and Christy stopped briefly beside the unknown couple's fresh graves. She did not pray for them in words, would not have known what to say. Instead, she imagined the pair rising into the light, hand in hand, and with that picture in her mind a certain peace came over her. Holding a rapidly recovering Jenny in the familiar sling, Christy turned her back on death and set her thoughts and her heart on life.

They camped beside the lake that night, and while Christy and Jenny slept, huddled together under the blanket he provided, Zachary sat up, keeping watch. It was cold, and they went without food, not daring to light a fire lest they attract unwanted attention. The following day, around noon, the town of Primrose Creek sprang up in the distance.

"Do you suppose she's still contagious?" Christy asked Zachary. Jenny was smiling up at her from inside the sling, eyes bright, even after sleeping on the ground with no fire to warm her and jostling along on the back of a horse for the better part of two days.

"I doubt it," Zachary answered. "What do you want to do with her?"

Christy's heart swelled in her chest, threatening to break right in two. "I suppose that old woman will come for her pretty soon. It's going to be hard to give her up."

"She belongs with her own people," Zachary said reasonably. "You know that."

She nodded, then looked directly into his eyes. "Knowing something isn't the same as believing it," she said.

"Amen to that," he replied, and both of them knew they weren't talking about Jenny anymore.

Caney came to meet them as they crossed the meadow toward the lodge. She wiped both hands on her apron and narrowed her eyes. "Ain't you a sight," she said to Christy in a scolding tone that conveyed an equal amount of relief, as she held out her arms. "Let's have a look-see at that baby."

Christy surrendered Jenny to her old friend, watched as Caney peeled back the sling and peered at the child for a long time before speaking again. "Well, now. First I've seen of scarlet fever in a while. But she's on her way back, that's for sure."

Christy got down from the mare's back, while Zachary remained mounted and silent. The brim of his hat cast his features into shadow, and so she could not see his eyes, but she was intensely aware of him, all the same. She could, in fact, feel his regard in every nook and corner of her being. "Is it safe to take her to the lodge with Megan there?"

Caney fixed her with a level gaze. "I reckon so, but it seems likely to me that this little papoose's own people will want her back sooner instead of later. Indians cherish their children, you know."

Biting her lower lip, Christy nodded. She had had Jenny in her care for such a short time, less than two days, in fact, and yet she'd become deeply and permanently attached to the child in that time. She wanted to keep her, raise her as her own, though she knew that was impossible.

Caney looked up at Zachary. "I appreciate your lookin' after my girl here," she said with a slight toss of her head to indicate Christy. "Bringin' her home safe and all."

"Ma'am," he affirmed, with a tug at his hat brim.

That was all, just "Ma'am," and not a word to Christy. He simply bent from the saddle to gather the mare's dangling reins in one hand and rode away, headed toward town. He was out of sight before Christy realized that she hadn't thanked him.

"Come on back to the house now," Caney commanded gently, taking Christy's arm and at the same time retaining a secure hold on the baby. "I want to hear all about how you tended this baby. 'Sides, you're wanting a bath, a hot meal, and a good night's rest, by my reckoning."

Christy could only nod, and even as they started toward the lodge, she was still watching the place where Zachary had disappeared onto the road to town.

At home, Caney took care of her as though she were a child, sending Megan and Skye across the creek to borrow Bridget's bathtub. When she was clean and clad in a flannel nightgown, Christy consumed a bowl of stew, telling the grim story between bites. She climbed into her hay bale bed and fell into a deep and mercifully dreamless sleep.

When she awakened, it was morning, and Caney was singing to baby Jenny as she spooned something into her mouth. Jenny laughed up at her between bites, as if trying to join in. Christy's heart constricted, but she managed a smile and what she hoped was a cheerful tone.

"Good morning," she said.

Caney gave her a smile tinged with sadness. " 'Mornin', missy," she said. "This sweet thing here is in fine fettle today." She wriggled a small toe between two fingers, prompting more gurgling glee from Jenny. "Ain't you, darlin' girl?"

Christy was glad of Jenny's recovery, of course. It was something of a miracle, since scarlet fever was so often fatal, but it still meant letting go, and she wasn't looking forward to that. She'd had to let go of so much in her lifetime, so many people, so many places, so many things.

After dishing up a bowl of cornmeal flavored with molasses and handing it to Christy, Caney broached the subject they had both avoided until then. "You mean to tell me what really happened on that trip, or do I have to guess?"

Christy looked away, blinked, looked back. She knew Caney was asking if a romance had developed between her and Zachary, but she pretended not to understand. "I've already told you. The missionaries—the Arrons—were dead when we got there. Massacred. Zachary—Marshal Shaw—buried them, and we passed the night in their cabin. The morning after, we set out for home."

Caney's lips moved in what Christy knew was a private prayer for the Arrons, but the expression in her dark eyes was a relentless one. "Nothing happened? Between you and the marshal?"

A hot blush moved up Christy's neck to pulse in her cheeks. "Of course not," she said, perhaps too fiercely.

"It don't necessarily have to be physical, you know, for something to happen between a man and a woman. There's deeper things than makin' love, and I suspect you know that, even though you've been sheltered for most of your life. Things that fix one person in somebody's heart for good."

Christy shifted uncomfortably and lost all appetite for her cornmeal mush. The hay bales prickled her bottom and the backs of her thighs, even through her nightgown and the quilt beneath her. "I haven't changed my mind about marrying Jake, if that's what you're trying to find out."

Caney sighed, rocking the baby distractedly in her capable arms. "I reckon he might have changed his mind about you, though. Everybody in town knows you and the marshal were alone together all that time. A thing like that stirs up talk, Christy, right or wrong."

She nodded. What would she do if she'd alienated Jake for good? Too much depended on her making a successful marriage, and the timber baron was the only suitable candidate, for her present purposes, at least.

She was developing a headache and rubbed both temples in a vain attempt to forestall it. "Will you look after Jenny for me, Caney? Please? I need to speak with Mr. Vigil as soon as possible."

"I should say you do," Caney agreed, somewhat tartly. Her glance was fond, though, when she returned her attention to the baby. "So you're called Jenny, are you? Ain't that an interestin' thing? I knew another Jenny one time."

Christy ignored her friend's remark, arose, and

pulled on a wrapper to go down to the creek and wash. When she returned, face and hands stinging from the cold water, mind jolted into complete wakefulness by that same chill, she dressed very carefully. She wore an apricot silk, which she knew was flattering, if a little frayed at the hem and cuffs, and pinned her hair up in a loose bun at the back of her head. Although she dared not paint her face, she did go so far as to put the merest touch of rouge on her mouth.

"I declare," Caney remarked, looking her over. "If I didn't know better, I'd think you were a hussy, plain and simple."

Color pounded in Christy's cheeks—no doubt, that would be an improvement, given the fact that she'd been pale since the harrowing discovery at the mission three days before—but she did not stoop to offer a retort. The look she gave Caney was eloquent enough, anyhow.

Leaving the lodge, Christy met Megan.

"Where are you going?" Megan asked, looking shocked. "You look like you're dressed for a dance, and here it is barely breakfast time!"

Given that Christy was trying hard to do the best thing for all of them, her sister's confrontational attitude irritated her not a little. "I have business in town," she said, perhaps a bit pettishly.

Megan's hands went to her hips. She was a McQuarry, after all, and she could be as hard-headed as any of the rest of them. "What sort of 'business' could you possibly have, wearing a dress like that and rouge on your mouth?"

"It needn't concern you," Christy said. "Now, please get out of my way. I have two miles to walk, and I'd like to get started." She tried not to think of the renegade Paiutes who had so ruthlessly murdered the Arrons, and how they might be lurking in the nearby woods, even now. She couldn't afford to let fear get the better of her; if anything, the grisly scene at the mission had left her more convinced than ever that Megan belonged in San Francisco or some other relatively civilized city.

Megan remained squarely in Christy's path. "You've set your cap for Jake Vigil," she accused, as though it were a sin.

Christy lifted her chin. Her face felt hot with indignation, and her tone was crisp. "What if I have?"

"He's the wrong man," Megan insisted. She looked like Granddaddy in that moment, with her green eyes snapping and her jaw set. "What's worse, you know it!"

"That," Christy said, trying to go around her sister, "will be quite enough."

Megan immediately blocked her way again. "If you're doing *any part* of this on my account, Christy McQuarry," she said, "you're making a terrible mistake. I'm not a child, and I've got plans of my own!"

Christy was taken aback, to say the least. "What sort of plans?" she asked in a softer voice. *Dear God, don't let her say she wants to marry Caleb Strand or some other lumberjack. She's too young, too innocent, too fragile for such a life.*

"Never you mind what plans," Megan replied. "I'll

tell you this much, though—they don't include teaching school, and I've had all the book-learning I want, so if you're thinking of putting me into another school like St. Martha's, forget it. I won't waste my time studying Latin and embroidery with a lot of stupid society girls!"

Megan's words struck Christy like a slap in the face. Her sister didn't know what she was saying, of course, what she would be giving up. Surely, she could not possibly understand what it meant to battle the soil and the elements for a living, to do for a husband and children day and night.

"Excuse me," Christy said, and swept past Megan to start the long and dusty walk to town. Megan didn't understand the situation, that was all. At sixteen, she was still more child than woman. In time, she would thank Christy for keeping everyone's best interests in mind and pursuing them despite everything.

Jake looked Christy over without smiling when she stepped into his office more than an hour later. Her shoes were pinching and her pride was stung, for a whole nest of reasons, and she was in no mood to put up with a lot of nonsense.

"Are you going to invite me to sit down, or must I stand throughout the interview?" she asked.

"Sit down," Jake said, still not smiling. He was dressed in work clothes—a blue chambray shirt, open at the throat, and well-fitted denim pants. He was very attractive—why didn't that move her, even a little? Why didn't she want him the way she wanted Zachary Shaw?

She sat, folded her hands in her lap. Her backbone was straight as a broomstick. She knew she looked her very best, even after a two-mile walk, but that was little comfort in the face of Jake's dark countenance. She'd planned a speech and rehearsed it as she marched along, as much to keep from thinking about Indians as to prepare herself, but now she couldn't remember a single word. Pity. She recalled the substance of the argument as very convincing.

"Well?" Jake prompted. He drew back the chair behind his desk with a grating sound and sat down. "I have a business to run here, Miss McQuarry. If you wouldn't mind getting to the point—"

"Nothing happened," she said, and immediately turned scarlet.

"You spent several days and nights in the mountains with another man. *That* happened."

"We had to go, don't you see?" Christy demanded, getting angry. She had not expected Jake to be so stubborn, any more than she had expected Megan to behave in a fashion that could only be described as ungrateful. "The baby had scarlet fever—she needed a real doctor. I was trying to get help for her, and Zachary—Marshal Shaw—would not permit me to make the journey alone."

Jake leaned forward in his chair, his eyes flashing. He looked even more handsome in a temper than usual, but Christy might have been looking at a fine stallion or a spectacular painting, for all the passion she felt. "*I* would have gone," he said.

"I know," Christy confessed, losing some of her aplomb. "It's just that it all seemed so urgent at the time, and Mr. Shaw was right there with a horse for me to ride—"

"I'll just bet he was," Jake said, but she could tell that he was beginning to relent a little. He desired her with the same intensity as she desired Zachary, that was plain. She hoped it would be enough to sustain them both through the long years ahead.

"We have an understanding, you and I," she said. "I would never do anything to compromise either your honor or mine."

He gave a great sigh and tilted his head back, as though to stretch his neck. When he looked at Christy again, his eyes were smiling. "I believe that," he said, and opened a drawer in his desk.

Christy stiffened but managed a somewhat rigid smile in return. "Thank you," she said in a rather pointed tone.

He laid a diamond ring between them; its many stones gleamed and glittered in the dusty light pouring in through the window behind and above his head. "I've had this awhile. In case I found somebody to marry."

He looked and sounded like a small boy, proudly revealing a treasure, and Christy felt a stab of guilty dread. "It's—it's beautiful," she said.

He picked it up, came around the side of the desk, and took her hand. She managed to smile when he slipped it onto her finger, but it burned her flesh like a brand. She felt like a harlot, accepting payment for some unseemly act.

"Now it's official," he said, patting her hand once. "Just in case anybody has any doubts."

"Yes," Christy said. "It's official." She was glad she was still sitting down, because she felt faint. *Don't do this,* screamed a voice in her mind, a voice she recognized as her own.

He dropped to one knee beside her, holding her hand. "You'll never regret marrying me, Christy," he promised huskily. "I swear it."

She could only nod. The truth was, she hadn't even gone through with the ceremony yet, and she was *already* full of regrets. She rose shakily to her feet.

"Are you all right?" Jake asked, frowning.

"Just—just happy," she said.

He beamed. "I'm glad. I'll have someone hitch up the buggy, and then I'll drive you home myself, if you're ready to leave."

"I'd like to l-look at the house," she murmured. She needed something, in those desperate moments, to sustain her, to help keep up her resolve. "You wouldn't mind, would you?"

He looked enormously pleased. "No," he said. "Of course not. You'll be wanting changes, I imagine."

She looked away, saw through the plain timber walls of Jake's office to the street and the marshal's office beyond. "I imagine," she agreed, almost sighing the words.

Jake didn't seem to notice her reticence. No doubt, he was only seeing what he wanted to see, like most other people. "I don't guess it would be entirely proper, our being alone in the house before we're actually married. It isn't locked, though. You just go right in."

She nodded, somehow found the door and opened it, stepped outside. The walk to Jake's house was a short one, but it might have been a hundred miles, or a thousand, her feet—not to mention her heart—were so heavy.

She entered the mansion through the kitchen, a huge room with an indoor water supply, a massive and gleaming stove, a big pinewood table with eight chairs, and cupboards with doors. The floor, fashioned of lacquered wood, was dusty but otherwise beautiful, and a good washing would make it shine.

From there, Christy proceeded to the dining room, which she had seen the night of Jake's party. The large parlor was just off the entryway, and it boasted a white marble fireplace that must have cost the earth, though there were only a few pieces of furniture. Christy tried to imagine herself sewing beside a winter fire while Jake read a newspaper in the chair next to hers, but she couldn't.

She explored his study next; it was opposite the parlor and lined with floor-to-ceiling bookshelves. It was enlightening to see that Jake enjoyed reading, and mildly comforting, too. At least they had that much in common. Surely, they could build on a shared love of books and other quiet joys.

The staircase was a wide and graceful curve of gleaming wooden steps, and Christy climbed slowly, as though on her way to her own hanging. Perhaps Megan, young as she was, was right. Perhaps she was taking too much upon herself and making a dreadful mistake in the process.

The upstairs hallway was long and wide, with three doors on one side, three at the other, and a double set at the far end. Christy peeked into each bedroom, all of which were empty, before coming to stand before the towering doors of what she knew must be Jake's room.

Heart thumping, feet leaden, she finally turned one of the brass knobs and pushed the door open a little way. She closed her eyes, took a deep breath, and stepped over the threshold. It should have been Jake's scent that came to meet her, but instead it was Zachary's.

A tear slipped down her right cheek. The bed was a four-poster, intricately carved and set high off the floor. There was another marble fireplace, this one green and black, and at least two of the paintings on the walls were European. The curtains were Irish lace, and there were two gigantic wardrobes against one wall. Another door led to an astounding discovery—a stationary bathtub, commode, and sink. A contrivance at the foot of the tub served as a hot water reservoir. Christy discovered that the hard way, by touching the glittering, rattly thing and burning her fingers.

She was startled, to say the least, when she turned from the splendid bathroom to find herself facing the last person in the world she wanted to see just then.

"Maybe you ought to lie down on the bed," Zachary said, his eyes flashing with blue fire. "Make sure the mattress is to your liking."

She considered turning her back on him and walking off without a word, but that would be too much like running away. "Do you always walk into other people's houses uninvited?"

"Do you?"

"There's a difference," Christy informed him, with all the dignity she could muster. "I'm going to live here."

"That's the difference, all right," he snapped back, his nose so close to hers that she feared her eyes would cross.

She struggled to hold on to her temper and to keep from bursting into tears. "What do you want?" she demanded, and realized too late that the question had been an unfortunate one.

"You," Zachary answered. "I want you. And damn it, Christy, you want me."

"You're wrong!"

He took hold of her upper arms and lifted her almost onto her toes. "No," he rasped, "*you* are. God in heaven, Christy, don't do this. Don't do it to yourself, don't do it to Jake, don't do it to me!"

She was trembling all over and torn shamefully between flinging her arms around his neck to hold on for dear life and boxing his ears with both fists. "Get out," she hissed. "*Now.*"

He thrust out a sigh, and his splendid shoulders sagged a little. He let his hands fall to his sides. "All right," he said. "All right." Then, in complete contrast to his words, he pulled her into his arms again and kissed her so hard that she feared her mouth would be bruised. Worse still, she reveled in that forbidden kiss, surrendered to it, even moaned a little because it roused such a ferocious wanting in her.

When he put her away from him, she realized she was weeping, something only he could make her do. "Good-bye, Zachary," she said. "*Good-bye*."

He gazed at her for a long, telling moment, then turned and walked out. She heard his boot heels on the stairs and barely kept herself from running after him.

"Let this be over," she murmured to herself. "Please, God, let this be over."

"He's gone." Bridget seemed to take a sort of furious pleasure in delivering the news the next morning. "I hope you're happy now."

"Who's gone?" Christy asked, though she feared she knew.

"Zachary. He swore in a deputy yesterday afternoon and rode out with a wad of wanted posters in his saddle bags. Gus told Trace all about it last night at the town council meeting."

Wanted posters. She was sick at her stomach, and her knees felt weak. Zachary was going after outlaws, men sought for terrible crimes, and he might very well be killed. In those moments, she would have done almost anything to bring him back safe, but of course that was impossible. There was nothing she could do now but brazen things through. "That," she said, putting on a performance, "is no concern of mine. Zachary is a grown man, and he makes his own choices."

"That's true," Bridget said, still flushed with righteous anger, "except that we both know why he's doing this—don't we, Christy?"

She turned her back on her cousin; that seemed preferable to snatching her hair out by the roots. "I can't imagine what you're talking about."

"I could fertilize my petunia patch with *that* answer," Bridget persisted. "So help me, God, Christy, if he's shot because of your fancies of wealth and comfort, there won't be a person in Primrose Creek who'll speak to you ever again!"

Christy closed her eyes, shaken through and through, not by the prospect of ostracism—she'd experienced that at St. Martha's and survived just fine, thank you—but by an image of Zachary lying dead on some lonely trail, awash in his own blood. A chill went through her, and she hugged herself against it. When she offered no reply, Bridget spun her around to face her.

If Bridget hadn't been so completely pregnant, Christy might have forgotten all her personal compunctions concerning violence and tied in, kicking and scratching.

"Don't you *ever* do that again!" she cried. "You won't *always* be pregnant, you know!"

Bridget was undaunted and absolutely furious. "You're just like your father!" she spat.

"And you're just like yours!" Christy responded.

"Now, that's right grown-up," Caney put in from somewhere in the pulsing haze that seemed to surround the two cousins. "I reckon you'll be puttin' out your tongues next."

The reprimand dispelled some of the hostility, and Christy and Bridget stepped back from each other, although their fists were still clenched.

Caney stepped between them. "Bridget, you git on home before you work yourself up into a pet and cause that baby to let go afore its time. Christy, you go on with whatever you were up to before Bridget showed up, and hold your tongue. If you're like anybody, the pair of you, it's your old granddaddy, and that's your trouble right there. You're too much alike."

Too much like Bridget? Christy quelled an unladylike desire to spit, but she minded Caney's orders and continued with what she'd been doing—wringing out Jenny's diapers and draping them over various bushes to dry in the hot, dazzling sunshine.

They arrived in the middle of the afternoon, at least twenty mounted Paiute braves, painted for war and armed with spears, bows, and rifles. The sight of them brought back bloody memories of Reverend and Mrs. Arron, butchered in the sanctity of their own home.

Caney usually kept a shotgun somewhere within reach, and that day was no exception. She picked up the weapon and cocked it, and that gesture, coupled with the hard set of her face, sent a clear message that she meant business. Megan stood gaping in awe, and when Christy had recovered enough to hear anything but the thundering beat of her own pulse, she caught her sister's delighted exclamation.

"Zounds! *Indians!*"

They were going to die, Christy thought, with a peculiar sense of calm that resonated within her like an arrow quivering in its target. They'd never see another sunrise, any of them. Never laugh or argue. Never taste fried chicken or cold spring water.

She walked toward the Indians, heard Megan's gasp and Caney's muttered curse, and was only mildly relieved to see the old woman who had brought her Jenny, riding to the fore, her long gray braid dangling over one shoulder.

"Singing Deer—she is well?"

Singing Deer, Christy repeated to herself. So that was Jenny's true name. "Yes," she said, though a lump had formed in her throat and her eyes burned so badly that they might have been on fire.

"Bring," commanded the ancient one. That she enjoyed a position of authority in her tribe there could be no doubt. The painted braves, Christy realized, were in attendance to enforce her decrees, that was all, and probably would have preferred to be elsewhere.

Christy nodded, turned, and went into the lodge. Jenny—Singing Deer—was lying happily in a basket atop the bed, diapered and clean and very fascinated with the toes on her right foot. Christy had known this moment was coming, of course, but she still felt as though she'd been dealt a knee-breaking blow. In the short time she had had the child in her care, she had fallen in love with her. Now, she would probably never see her again.

Tenderly, she lifted Singing Deer from her basket,

wrapped her in a clean blanket she could not really spare, and carried her outside.

The elderly woman leaned down to collect the child. Her granddaughter, perhaps, or even her great-granddaughter.

Christy surrendered her charge unflinchingly, although inside she was falling apart. "She likes potato broth," she said, without intending to speak at all. It was unlikely that the visitors understood what she'd said or would have cared if they had.

The woman nodded, her gaze level. She barked out a few words in the language of her people, and one of the braves thrust a feathered spear into the ground at Christy's feet with enough force to make her start. She sensed, rather than saw, that Caney had raised her shotgun, ready to fire.

"No!" Christy cried, with one look backward. "Caney, don't shoot!"

A brisk exchange took place between the woman and several of the fiercer braves. Then, at her command, the party turned their ponies and rode away, vanishing into the timber.

"Wait until I tell Skye about *this,"* Megan enthused, reaching for the staff of the spear with the obvious intention of pulling it up to use as an exhibit.

"Leave it," Christy said.

Megan looked at her in surprise. Caney was standing close by, one hand under Christy's left elbow, the other clasping the shotgun.

"But it's an Indian spear," Megan said, with as much wonder as if the thing were the Holy Cross itself.

"Exactly," Christy managed to gasp. Then she dropped to her knees in the tall grass, covered her face with both hands, and sobbed with sorrow and relief and any number of other emotions.

Caney was soon kneeling beside her, gathering her into her arms. "There, now. You go right ahead and cry, Miss Christy. You go right on ahead. Lord knows, you have all the reason in the world."

"Why can't I have the spear?" Megan persisted.

"Because it's a sign to other Indians, that's why," Caney replied. "I reckon it means 'stay away.' Now, go fetch me some creek water and a clean cloth. Can't you see your sister needs tendin'?"

Christy was beginning to recover a little; her sobs had turned to hiccoughs, and she didn't need to cling quite so tightly to Caney.

"What is it, child?" Caney asked with a gruff gentleness that made Christy want to start wailing again. "I know you didn't expect to keep that sweet little baby. You couldn't have."

Christy nodded. She'd known this would happen, of course, but that didn't make it one bit easier. She'd lost Jenny, and Zachary had ridden off somewhere, looking to get himself killed. The future looked bleak indeed, a long series of black and empty days and endless lonely nights.

Chapter 7

Jake Vigil proved to be a patient man. He waited through what remained of April and all of May. He brought Christy flowers he'd gathered himself, took her for moonlight drives in his smart, gleaming buggy, and sent all the way to Chicago for his wedding gift to her, a grand piano.

All that time, Christy was in torment, and not merely because of the fruitlessness of her continuing efforts to fall truly in love with her future husband. Zachary had been gone for weeks, and as far as she knew, no one had heard from him. Christy had bad dreams nearly every night, dreams in which Zachary had been shot dead by one of the monstrous men he was hunting.

One night in early June, when Caney was in town courting Mr. Hicks, Trace came running across the footbridge and up the hillside, shouting for Christy.

She had been sitting on a stone near the creek, brushing her hair and planning to retire early and read one of a stack of books she'd borrowed from Jake's library. Sometimes, though not always, filling her mind with someone else's words served as a talisman of sorts, keeping the nightmares at bay.

"What is it?" she asked, even though she thought she already knew.

Trace didn't wait for her to rise; he grabbed one of her hands and wrenched her to her feet. "Bridget's having pains, real close together. She says the baby's coming."

Christy drew a deep breath to steady herself, let it out slowly. She had assisted Caney in the delivery of several babies on the wagon train but never actually brought one into the world herself. "I'll go to her right now," she said calmly, though inwardly she was considerably less composed than she must have seemed to Trace. "You head into town and fetch Caney back. She'll be with Mr. Hicks."

Trace shook his head. "I'm not leaving my wife," he said, and it was plain by his tone that he meant it. "Skye's off somewhere, with Noah, like most times. She can go, soon as she gets back."

Christy followed him back across the creek and into the sprawling house. Bridget was still dressed and pacing back and forth in front of the hearth.

Although relations had been strained between the two cousins, to say the least, Christy put everything aside and took Bridget's arm. "Trace says it's time."

Bridget smiled weakly and nodded. "Yes," she said. "It's going to be quicker than it was with Noah, I think. I felt the first pain about an hour ago, and now they're pretty hard, with just a few seconds in between."

Christy returned her cousin's smile. "Let's get down to business, then," she said, and turned to address Bridget's pale, wide-eyed husband. She had to admire him for insisting on staying, when he was obviously scared half out of his skin. "Trace, I'll need plenty of hot water. And you'll probably want to send Skye and Noah over to our place if they show up. There's no time to fetch Caney."

He nodded, grabbed up two buckets, and stumbled out of the cabin like a sleepwalker, headed for the creek.

Meanwhile, Christy escorted Bridget into the bedroom she and Trace shared, helped her out of her clothes, into a loose nightgown, and into bed.

"Are you scared?" Christy asked quietly, rolling up the sleeves of her dress. There was water in the pitcher on the washstand; she poured some into the basin and began to scrub her hands with yellow soap Bridget had probably made herself.

Bridget nodded. "A little," she confessed.

"I know how to do this," Christy said quietly in an effort to reassure her. "Caney taught me when we were with the wagon train."

Bridget nodded again. And then the pains intensified; she doubled up in bed and moaned aloud.

Christy examined her gently. It would not be long, judging by appearances. In fact, they'd be fortunate if Trace got the water heated in time to be of any help.

"H-have you and Jake set a date yet?" Bridget asked.

Christy ached. *Zachary,* her heart cried, in silent

sorrow. For a while, she'd played a game with herself. If Zachary returned, either penniless or prospering, and if he still wanted her, she would take it as a sign from God and marry him in spite of everything. But he hadn't come back, and time was running out. Jake wasn't willing to wait forever.

"Yes," she said without meeting Bridget's eyes. "We'll be married this coming Sunday, before church. Reverend Taylor has already agreed to perform the ceremony."

Bridget gasped as a particularly grievous pain seized her, knotting her belly with such force that the musculature was visible even through the fabric of her nightgown. "You're—you're sure?"

"I'm sure," Christy said. It wasn't precisely true, of course, but the charade might as well begin now as on her wedding day, just a few days hence. "Now, let's talk about you. Would you like something to hold on to? I could tie sheets to the bedposts."

Bridget shook her head. "I-I don't think I'm going to need anything like that. The baby seems to have made up its mind."

Christy smiled. When she examined Bridget again, she saw the crown of a tiny head. "You *are* quick," she said.

Bridget lay back on her pillows, panting. "Trace—is so scared—"

"Don't worry about Trace," Christy said. "I gave him some busywork to keep him out from underfoot. He'll be all right."

Bridget's back arched, and she gave a rasping cry.

"Push," Christy ordered.

Bridget pushed.

"Again." A small, perfectly formed head appeared, sporting masses of spiky golden hair. Christy's heart soared, and she smiled, despite the inherent drama of the situation. "Almost finished, Bridge. One more push."

The baby slipped out with the next contraction, but Bridget's belly was still distended. So Caney had been right; no surprise there. Bridget was indeed carrying twins.

"It's a boy," Christy said, making sure the baby's mouth and nose were clear and then tying off and severing the cord.

Bridget looked down, her face glistening with sweat. "Oh, God," she moaned, "there's another one."

"So it would appear," Christy replied, just as Trace bumbled into the room. "The water's about ready," he said.

Christy handed him his son, unwashed and hastily bundled into a towel, and turned back to Bridget, who was yelling in earnest by then.

His eyes widened with the realization that Bridget was about to give birth to a second baby. "Maybe it's crosswise," Trace said, looking down at his wife with a combination of joy, bewilderment, and worry, but keeping a secure hold on the babe in his arms.

Christy might have laughed if she hadn't been so busy. "Look after your son," she said. "We're a little busy with number two, here."

The girl arrived five minutes later, as blond and

perfect as her brother, and Bridget finally was allowed to lie still, struggling for breath, mussed and bloody and beaming with happiness.

Christy attended to the necessary details, changed the bedsheets without dislodging Bridget, in just the way Caney had taught her to do, and quietly left the room so that Bridget and Trace could be alone with each other and the two new additions to the family.

She washed thoroughly at the kitchen washstand, though she supposed her dress was unsalvageable, and wept silently because no matter how many babies she bore Jake Vigil, she would never have what Bridget and Trace were sharing at that moment, in the very room where they had conceived their babies.

In time, she noticed the familiar McQuarry family Bible, a large volume, awaiting the day's date—June 10—and the names of the newcomers, now squalling lustily on the other side of the parlor wall. With a reflective smile, she sat down, placed the Bible in her lap, and opened it to the pages of records in front.

The tome had been printed during the American Revolution, and it had probably cost a fortune, books being rare and very precious in that time.

Thinking of home, of Granddaddy, of Virginia, Christy ran an index finger down the long, long list of names. Births, deaths, marriages. McQuarrys all. When she reached her own generation, her breath caught in her throat, and she blinked, certain that she could not have read the copperplate handwriting correctly.

But she had.

With a snap, Christy closed the McQuarry Bible on a secret that had been right there all the time, in plain English, and she was still staring into space, assimilating all the ramifications, when Trace came out, beaming with pride, to say Bridget and the babies were sleeping.

"Did—did you decide what to call them?" she asked.

He nodded, went to wash his hands, then poured coffee for them both and came to sit in the second rocking chair in front of the fireplace. "The boy is Gideon Mitchell, the girl Rebecca Christina."

Under any other circumstances, Christy might have resented the fact that Bridget had just laid claim to two of the best family names. Yet Bridget had given the girl Christy's own, which was surely an olive branch of sorts, and Christy was still reeling from what she'd just discovered in the pages of the McQuarry Bible.

Granddaddy, she thought, with the beginnings of a smile, *you crafty old devil, you.*

Sunday morning arrived all too soon, and Christy, still keeping her discovery to herself, still debating over whether or not to reveal it to anyone, ever, dressed for her marriage with all the exuberance Marie Antoinette must have felt when grooming herself for the guillotine.

"You can still back out, you hear?" Caney hissed as she helped Christy with the pale blue silk gown they had altered to serve as a wedding dress. They were in a corner of Reverend Taylor's tent church, behind an improvised changing screen. The parishioners would not arrive until later, after the deed had been done.

Christy sighed. Zachary hadn't returned, which surely meant that she ought to go ahead with her plans. "Where is Megan?" she fussed. "I declare, if she's late, I'll wring her neck."

"Don't you fret, now. Miss Skye will bring her right along," Caney said. "It's a pity Miss Bridget can't be here, too, but with them babies so new and all—"

Christy didn't mind not having a large wedding; the two people she needed for support, Caney and Megan, would be there. As far as she was concerned, no other witnesses were necessary, or even desirable. She felt like someone about to commit a crime.

A stir beyond the changing screen alerted her to the arrival of her bridegroom; she peeked around and swallowed hard at the sight of Jake, so handsome in his new suit of clothes. He was accompanied by Trace, who would serve as his best man, and several of the men who worked with him in the timber enterprise.

Apparently sensing Christy's regard, he looked up, met her gaze, and smiled.

Christy dodged behind the screen again. How could she do this? How? Jake was a decent man; he deserved a woman who truly loved him. "Caney—" she began.

Caney's expression was eager. "What, baby?"

She thought of the big house, the money, the opportunities and security she and Megan would both enjoy because of this union. "Nothing," she said, sighing the word.

Overhead, an unseasonable rain began to patter on the roof of the large tent. The weather was certainly in keeping with Christy's state of mind.

The sound of a fiddle playing the opening strains of the wedding march signaled the beginning of the ceremony. Caney fussed with Christy's hair and dress for a few more seconds, then pushed her around the edge of the screen.

Megan was standing near the altar, looking like one of the Three Graces, a bouquet of yellow and pink wildflowers clasped in both hands. Reverend Taylor was in position, prayer book in hand, and Jake stood to his left, gazing fondly at Christy, urging her forward with his eyes.

She swallowed, hesitated, took one step and then another. Somehow reached his side, although she could not feel her feet touching the sawdust-covered floor, could not feel anything except her knotted stomach.

The rain pounded at the tent top, and thunder crashed high above their heads. Jake's arm brushed Christy's, and he smelled pleasantly of some fine gentleman's cologne. She squeezed her eyes shut and opened them again just as quickly. She prayed she wouldn't disgrace herself and Jake by fainting right there in front of God and creation.

"Dearly beloved," the reverend began solemnly, "we are gathered here—"

Christy bit her upper lip.

"—in the sight of God—"

"No!" she burst out. She looked up at Jake's bewildered face. "I'm sorry," she whispered. "I'm so sorry. But I can't do this. I can't!" With that, she lifted her skirts, turned, and fled between the rows of rough-hewn pews toward the large, open doorway of the tent. She ran out into the hammering rain, through the downpour, through the gummy mud and the puddles, utterly heedless of everything except the need to escape and with no particular destination in mind.

He was tired, he was wet to the skin, and, apparently, he was hallucinating. Christy was running toward him, head down, wearing what looked like a wedding gown. He reined in the stallion, waited, and watched. She hadn't seen him yet; that was the only conclusion he could draw with any certainty, for the moment at least.

As she neared, he stepped down from the saddle and flung the reins loosely over the hitching rail in front of Diamond Lil's. He'd been gone for weeks, sleeping on the ground, solemnly working his way through the stack of wanted posters he'd gathered from the walls of the marshal's office. He'd earned a considerable sum since he'd been away, but with all that time to think, he'd had no choice but to face things about himself that he might not have looked at otherwise.

First of all, he'd explored the troubling fact that he was not only willing to marry a woman who would have him only if he had money in the bank, but half crazed with the need, and he'd asked himself if he truly cared that much. The answer was yes, and that hadn't changed, but at some point he'd made a decision: he wouldn't sell his soul, not even for Christy. No matter how badly it hurt to turn away, he wasn't going to buy her love.

Now, watching her running toward him through the rain, he was thoroughly bemused. He was also fairly certain she was going to run right into Jack Findley's hay wagon and do herself serious injury.

He stepped into her path and caught her upper arms firmly in both hands, lest she fall. Rain danced all around them, falling hard enough to raise a crackling sound from the roofs of Primrose Creek's few buildings.

She looked up at him in disbelief. "Zachary?"

He smiled. "Yup," he said. "Somebody chasing you?"

She must have known he was teasing, but the expression in her eyes was bruised, wary. She shook her head. "I love you," she said.

He felt as though he'd fallen out of a hayloft and landed stomach-first on an anvil. "What?"

"I love you!" she yelled over the rain.

He laughed, mostly because he could not contain the swell of joy that rose up inside him as her words hit home. Just as quickly, he summoned up a stern expression. "What about Jake?"

"I can't marry him. You were right. It would be wrong, even cruel." Her hair was soaked, and if he bided his time, he figured he might see her dress turn transparent.

He took her arm and pulled her swiftly out of the street, along the board sidewalk of which the town council was justifiably proud, and into his office. Fortunately, the deputy was nowhere around.

He took a blanket from one of the cots in the jail cell and wrapped her in it. There was coffee on the stove; he poured her a cup and added a generous dollop of bourbon. "Drink that," he ordered.

To his eternal surprise, she obeyed without question, her hands shivering as she closed both of them around the mug and lifted it to her lips. She looked like a drowned kitten, standing there sipping the worst coffee west of the Missouri, but he didn't dare soften his heart. Not yet. She, and she alone, possessed the power to rip it right out of his chest.

"Now, tell me what you were doing running down the middle of the street in the rain, wearing that fancy dress?"

She was trembling. "Today was supposed—supposed to be my wedding day."

"But you called it off."

She flushed, nodded guiltily. "Yes. In the end, I couldn't go through with it. I couldn't marry anybody for money."

He took off his sodden canvas coat and hung it from a peg on the wall. He'd been on the trail awhile, and he needed clean clothes, a shave, and a haircut. Not to mention a good meal and about twelve hours of uninterrupted sleep. "I see," he said.

She set the cup aside, came toward him, laid both hands on his chest, and looked up into his face. "I've hurt Jake, and you, too. I'm sorry, Zachary."

It took all his restraint to keep from hauling her against him and kissing her with all the accumulated passion of weeks on the road, when he'd hoped against hope that he'd get back to Primrose Creek before she went through with that fool scheme of hers.

"Now what?" he asked, mentally holding his breath.

"That's up to you," she answered, and he thought he saw her heart shining in those wondrous, stormy-sky eyes of hers. "If you can forgive me, then I'd like for us to start over. I don't care if we have to scrape for a living for the rest of our lives, as long as we can be together."

She didn't know about the money. Probably assumed he'd been unsuccessful, tracking stage robbers, murderers, and cattle rustlers. He felt lightheaded with happiness and new hope.

"I love you, Christy," he said. "And whatever I have, whether it's a little or a lot, I want to share it with you. Will you marry me?"

A beatific smile spread from her eyes to the rest of her face and finally seemed to glow from the very center of her being. She blinked away rainwater—or maybe tears—and reached up to touch his face. "Yes," she said. "Yes, I'll marry you. When?"

"How about now?" he heard himself ask. "The reverend was all set for a hitching anyhow. Might as well be us."

She nodded her agreement, but that sad look had slipped into her eyes again.

"I don't feel right, being so happy, when Jake is so—so—"

"Listen to me," he said, holding her shoulders now. Oh, to peel away that wet dress and the equally wet underthings beneath it, but he *would* wait. If it killed him—and he thought it might—he would wait. "Jake will be hurting for a while, that's true. But you did the right thing, Christy, for both of you. Marrying him wouldn't have been any favor, when you claim it's me you love."

She stood on tiptoe and kissed his chin. "I *do* love you," she said.

He kissed her in earnest then.

They were married that evening, in the front room at Bridget and Trace's place on Primrose Creek, with Megan, Skye, and Caney all in attendance and all beaming with approval. They would spend their wedding night in Skye's room, while she and Megan and Caney "camped" in the lodge across the stream.

It pleased Christy that Bridget was there, looking on with a happy smile. They still had their differences, and probably always would, but Granddaddy's entry in the family Bible had changed things, at least on Christy's part. Tomorrow, or the next day, she would broach the subject with her cousin, but for now, all that mattered was Zachary and the vows that would bind them forever.

* * *

The bed was wide, with a feather mattress, and the sheets were fresh and crisp. Rain whispered at the window and sputtered on the small hearth as Zachary closed the door on the rest of the world, loosening his tie as he turned toward Christy.

He shrugged out of his coat and tossed it aside, then crossed to where she stood, took her into his arms, and kissed her softly at first, then with an intensity that grew by degrees until it was blazing within them both, fusing into a single flame.

"No second thoughts," he said sleepily, his mouth still very close to hers, when the kiss was over, "about marrying a dirt-poor U.S. Marshal?"

She shook her head, sure of her answer. "No second thoughts. Kiss me again, Zachary. Now."

He chuckled and did as he was bidden. At the same time, he began unbuttoning the front of her dress—an ivory and lace affair borrowed from Bridget—and smoothed it down over her shoulders and arms. It caught at her waist and then dropped in a pool at her feet.

She trembled, standing there in her best underthings, so ready to give herself to this man and yet frightened because it was an utterly new experience, and she didn't know exactly what to expect.

"Don't be scared," he said in that same throaty voice. The firelight made an aura in his golden hair. "I'd never do anything to hurt you."

She inclined her head toward the closed door of the bedroom. "Do you think they—they know—?"

He laughed. "Yeah, they know."

She felt herself go crimson, not just in her face but all over. Of course, they were all aware of what was happening. What a foolish question. "Oh," she said.

"Forget about everybody else," Zachary said, and ran the backs of his fingers down her cheek, along her neck, over her collarbone, and onto the top of her breast. "Pretend there's nobody in the world but you and me."

It seemed easy enough to do, standing there in her drawers and camisole, with her husband's hand brushing and then claiming her breast in a delicate grasp that elicited a soft cry of pleasure. "You and me," she repeated drunkenly.

He blew out the lamp, so that the fire provided the only light, and began unbuttoning his shirt. Christy didn't trust her knees to support her; she sat down on the edge of the bed and watched as her shadowy bridegroom kicked off his boots, shrugged out of his shirt, began to unfasten his trousers. He was naked as a savage when he came to her, raised her gently to her feet, and removed the last of her garments.

For a long moment, he weighed her breasts in his hands, gazing reverently into her face. "God in heaven, Christy," he rasped. "I love you. And I need you so much."

She was too moved to speak. Too anxious. Too hungry.

He kissed her again and thereby dispensed with the last of her equilibrium. If he hadn't laid her gently down on the bed, she would have fallen, weak as a thin reed in a high wind.

More kisses followed, each one deeper and longer than the last, and then Zachary brushed the tender place under her ear with his lips, tasted her neck and the ridge of her collarbone. Then—

Christy cried out in ecstasy and clasped her hands behind his head, holding him close to her breast, delighting in every motion of his lips and tongue.

In time, he attended her other breast in the same way, and he was in no hurry about it. Christy lay tossing and writhing beneath him, urging him on with desperate little pleas, but he would not be rushed.

"Please," she whimpered.

He ran the tip of his tongue around her navel, and her hips sprang high off the bed, seemingly of their own accord. "Not yet," he said. "You need—to be ready."

She had no idea what he meant by "ready." If this state of frenzied wanting didn't qualify, there was no telling what she should expect.

She soon found out, and the pleasure was so fiery, so ferocious, that she turned her face into her pillow in order to muffle a moan that came from some heretofore uncharted region of her being. He drove her higher and higher, and on each plateau, just when she was sure she could not survive any more of this sweet tension, he added fuel to the fire.

Finally, in a devastating inner explosion, he brought her to a new place, a new part of herself that she had never known existed. The descent was excruciatingly slow, and she caught on small branches of delight as she passed, her hands damp where she clasped the rails of the headboard.

After what seemed like an eternity, Zachary poised himself over her, careful not to crush her with his weight. His eyes searched hers, asking a silent question, and she nodded, loving him as much for that question as she did for the answer.

He entered her carefully but in a single, decisive stroke. She clenched her fingers on his back at the brief pain, then was caught off guard by a fresh storm of sensation. Gratification took a long time, but when it came, it shattered them both, left them collapsed and breathless in each other's arms.

As tired as they were, the moon was setting when they finally slept.

Bridget was nursing little Gideon, her bosom covered by a baby blanket, while Rebecca, already fed, slept on her shoulder with an abandon only infants can manage. Summer sunshine glittered on the creek, and across the way, the sounds of hammers and saws punctuated the morning songs of birds and insects as work continued on the lodge, which was being turned into a real home, with rooms and floors and windows.

They had brought the two rocking chairs outside, and Christy was holding the family Bible on her lap. Her mother's cameo brooch, which Zachary had retrieved for her by paying her debt to Gus the storekeeper, was pinned to the bodice of her dress.

"I don't believe you," Bridget said, unsmiling.

"See for yourself," Christy replied, folding back the book's heavy cover.

Bridget leaned over, and her blue eyes widened as

she read. Read again. "Saints in suspenders," she marveled in a stunned whisper. "We're *sisters?* The four of us are sisters?"

Christy sighed and closed the Bible. "Yes," she said with a little sniff. "But we don't have to tell anybody." She paused. "Do we?"

More to treasure from

Linda Lael Miller

Angelfire
Banner O'Brien
Caroline and the Raider
Corbin's Fancy
Daniel's Bride
Desire and Destiny
Emma and the Outlaw
Fletcher's Woman
Knights
Lauralee
The Legacy
Lily and the Major
Memory's Embrace

MOON FIRE

MY DARLING MELISSA

MY OUTLAW

ONE WISH

PIRATES

PRINCESS ANNIE

SPRINGWATER

A SPRINGWATER CHRISTMAS

SPRINGWATER SEASONS:
RACHEL, SAVANNAH, MIRANDA, JESSICA

TAMING CHARLOTTE

TWO BROTHERS

THE VOW

WANTON ANGEL

WILLOW

THE WOMAN OF PRIMROSE CREEK:
BRIDGET, SKYE, MEGAN, CHRISTY

YANKEE WIFE

POCKET BOOKS

2804

DATE DUE

JUL 08 '00			
JUL 21 '00			
JUL 27 '00			
APR 23 '03			

Date June 2000

SEDRO-WOOLLEY PUBLIC LIBRARY

1. Materials checked out from the library may be kept for two weeks and renewed for another two weeks, unless otherwise approved.

2. A fine of ten cents a day will be charged for any library materials kept past the due date. No book will be issued to any person incurring such a fine until paid.

3. Library materials must be returned to the library in as good condition as when taken.

4. Patrons must pay for lost or mutilated books, records, or magazines.

5. Each borrower is held responsible for all books drawn on his card and for all fines accruing on the same.

DEMCO

8-30-02
Book ret from Newhalem